D0547949

"You can't walk

Gideon caught her by the arm.

"Stay away from me. You're jealous because a boy wants to walk out with me. No matter who it is, you find fault with them," Addy sputtered. "Even the butcher. You did everything you could to show him up for a pompous fuddy-duddy."

"He *was* a pompous fuddy-duddy."

"You know what?" She started walking again. Fast. "The trouble with you, Gideon Esch, is that you like me yourself. And you're too much of a coward to admit it!"

"*Ne!* That's not it," he protested, following her. "I'm just… I'm looking out for you. You deserve better than that boy, who isn't old enough to grow a proper beard."

"At least he's man enough to court a woman!"

That stopped him short in his shoes. "Addy…"

"Addy, nothing." She stopped and turned back to him. "If you'd be honest with yourself, you'd know that I'm speaking the truth." She started walking again. "I'm going home."

Gideon could do nothing but watch her go.

He always tried to be honest. But could he be so now? Could he admit she was right?

Emma Miller lives quietly in her old farmhouse in rural Delaware. Fortunate enough to be born into a family of strong faith, she grew up on a dairy farm, surrounded by loving parents, siblings, grandparents, aunts, uncles and cousins. Emma was educated in local schools and once taught in an Amish schoolhouse. When she's not caring for her large family, reading and writing are her favorite pastimes.

Books by Emma Miller

Love Inspired

The Amish Matchmaker
A Match for Addy

Hannah's Daughters
Courting Ruth
Miriam's Heart
Anna's Gift
Leah's Choice
Redeeming Grace
Johanna's Bridegroom
Rebecca's Christmas Gift
Hannah's Courtship

Visit the Author Profile page at Harlequin.com for more titles.

A Match for Addy

Emma Miller

HARLEQUIN LOVE INSPIRED®

If you purchased this book without a cover you should be aware
that this book is stolen property. It was reported as "unsold and
destroyed" to the publisher, and neither the author nor the
publisher has received any payment for this "stripped book."

Recycling programs
for this product may
not exist in your area.

LOVE INSPIRED BOOKS

ISBN-13: 978-0-373-04322-4

A Match for Addy

Copyright © 2015 by Emma Miller

All rights reserved. Except for use in any review, the reproduction or utilization of
this work in whole or in part in any form by any electronic, mechanical or other
means, now known or hereinafter invented, including xerography, photocopying
and recording, or in any information storage or retrieval system, is forbidden without
the written permission of the editorial office, Love Inspired Books, 233 Broadway,
New York, NY 10279 U.S.A.

This is a work of fiction. Names, characters, places and incidents are either the
product of the author's imagination or are used fictitiously, and any resemblance to
actual persons, living or dead, business establishments, events or locales is entirely
coincidental.

This edition published by arrangement with Love Inspired Books.

® and TM are trademarks of Love Inspired Books, used under license. Trademarks
indicated with ® are registered in the United States Patent and Trademark Office,
the Canadian Intellectual Property Office and in other countries.

www.Harlequin.com

Printed in U.S.A.

Behold, you are beautiful, my love; behold, you are beautiful.
                              —*Song of Solomon* 1:15

Chapter One

Kent County, Delaware...June

Dorcas Coblentz walked at a brisk pace, eager to reach Sara Yoder's farm. Today was going to be an exciting day; she could feel it. She just wished her mother hadn't insisted that she wear her church shoes to her new job. They were black leather oxfords, old-fashioned, heavy and exactly like the ones her *grossmama* wore. Dorcas understood the value of *Plain* shoes that would hold up to mud and rain, but these were more suited to a sixty-year-old woman than one less than half that age.

And they had rubbed a blister on the big toe of her left foot.

It didn't matter that they were the same size her *mam* had been buying for her since she was fourteen; this pair had never fit right. Dorcas had tried to explain the problem to her, but as long as she lived under her parents' roof, she would be allowed little choice in her own clothing. No one ever asked for her opinion on anything, and when she dared give it, she wasn't taken seriously. Martha and Reuben Coblentz believed that a girl's parents should make decisions for her until she moved into her husband's home. Then it was *his* responsibility to make those decisions. What was funny about that idea was that, as far as she could tell, it was her mother who made all the decisions in their house.

Dorcas sighed as she walked along the wooded path between her parents' property and Sara's. Dealing with her parents was becoming more and more frustrating. She should have been married years ago, like her pretty Yoder cousins. Then she would have had her own husband, household and children. It wasn't that she didn't love her parents or honor them, as the Bible told her she must. But every once in a while, Dorcas longed to have more independence. Almost as much as she longed for a beau.

That thought elicited another long sigh from Dorcas.

She'd just learned that chubby Barbara Beachy had a young man courting her, a man with his own horse and buggy. And Barbara was barely seventeen. Sunday, Barbara had confided in Dorcas that she should try prayer to find a husband. The thing was, Dorcas *had* been praying for one every night since she was fifteen. Maybe that was where she had made her mistake. Maybe it wasn't right to pray for a husband. Good health, rain, even patience—she could understand asking God for those things. But maybe bothering Him about a husband was irreverent. Maybe that's why she'd never had a boy ask her to a singing, or even offer her a ride home from a frolic.

Dorcas straightened her thin shoulders and walked a little faster. Now her right shoe was rubbing her heel, which took her mind off the left foot a little. She didn't want to be late on her first day at her new job. It was important to make a good impression on cousin Sara, who was new to Seven Poplars, and—her *mam* said—rich enough to set sausage, bacon and scrapple on her breakfast table every morning. Sara had offered to pay Dorcas well for her assistance in getting settled into her new house, and then, if things worked out, Dorcas would continue to help with cleaning and cooking on a regular basis.

Dorcas caught a flash of the hem of her dress and smiled to herself. Her shoes were awful, but at least she could be happy with her new dress. Her *mam* had paid cousin Johanna to sew it for her, and the material was the nicest that Dorcas had ever worn. It was the prettiest shade of lavender; she'd never had a lavender dress before. Her mother always chose dark colors for her. This morning, she had covered it with a full-length work apron. The fabric felt soft against her skin and made her smile every time she looked down at it.

Dorcas's own sewing wasn't that good. She supposed that she could have done a better job if their treadle machine didn't keep breaking the thread and grinding to a stop in the middle of a straight seam. Finances were tight in their home, and her *mam* said the old worn-out sewing machine was the least of their worries. Dorcas was glad to have an opportunity to help her family by working for Sara. Her *dat* had promised that she could keep part of her wages, and it was exciting to think that, for the first time ever, she'd have money to spend as she chose.

Dorcas intended to work hard for Sara and prove that picking her, when she could have had any of a dozen unmarried girls in Seven Poplars, had been the best choice. Dorcas had been so eager to start that she'd hurried through oatmeal, stewed prunes and coffee this morning, not even taking time for toast and apple butter. And wanting to be there early, she decided to cut through the woods by the old logging road rather than walk down the blacktop from their farm to Sara's place.

There was no gate at the end of the woods road, just a four-foot wire fence, overgrown in a morass of poison ivy, thorns and wild roses. There was an old wooden ladder, a stile, to get over it. Almost to the stile, Dorcas stopped and shifted her right foot inside her shoe. She was definitely working on a blister on her heel. She glanced up in indecision. It was another quarter of a mile to the farmhouse. How was that going to look to Sara if her new employee showed up for her first day of work limping like a foundered mare?

The clunky shoes just weren't going to do today.

Dorcas glanced around, hands on her hips. The path was used by plenty of the neighbors, but there was no one in sight. No one would ever know. She quickly untied her shoes, slipped out of them and removed her black stockings. Into the shoes the stockings went, then she put them behind a tree. They would be safe there, and she could retrieve them on her way home, without her mother being any the wiser.

With the grass delightfully cool beneath her feet, Dorcas gazed up at the fence. While the rungs on the stile were old and covered with moss, she knew she could easily climb them. Without any trouble, she scrambled up. She'd taken the first step on the far side when suddenly wood cracked under one foot. As she started to fall, Dorcas threw out her arms and windmilled, in an attempt to catch her balance. It was too late. She tumbled sideways and somehow fell headfirst into the tangle of fencing, vines and briars.

"Ach!" she cried as she hit the ground.

One shoulder had slammed into the wooden fence post as she went down, and for an instant, the wind was knocked out of her. Dorcas lay caught in a snare of green briars and stared up dizzily at the bright blue sky. How did these things happen to her? She was a good girl who obeyed her parents and tried to follow the laws of God. Things like this were not supposed to happen—not on the first day of work at her very first job!

Dorcas's right knee and the palm of her left hand burned; she was sure she'd cut herself on something. Her knee felt as though the flesh had been gouged, and she felt a warm trickle of blood.

Her eyes welled up suddenly, as much from disappointment as pain. Today was *not* supposed to go like this. Today was a new start. She'd decided that this morning when she'd risen from her morning prayers.

But Dorcas wasn't a crier. She'd learned long ago that tears didn't do a body a bit of good. She shoved her dress over her bare legs and tried to sit up, but the briars scratched her arms and legs, seeming to pull her down. The harder she tried to get up, the more it hurt. She lay back for a second to think. How was she going to get out of the hedgerow without further injuring herself? Maybe if she could get her feet beneath her, she could wiggle her way out. Dorcas rolled to one side, only to find that her skirt was snagged on a splinter of the fence post. She rolled onto her back and tried to free the material, but she couldn't work it loose. The only way she could get free, at this angle, would be to tear the dress off the post.

Her throat constricted. Now she *wanted* to cry. Her *mam* had warned her to wear her old burgundy-colored dress, but it was patched and scandalously short, sewn for her when she was younger and hadn't yet grown to such an unseemly height. She'd so badly wanted to wear the pretty new dress on her first day of work. Now she was paying the price for her vanity.

"Was in der welt?" It was a male voice.

Dorcas froze.

"Are you hurt?" He switched to English.

Dorcas tried wildly to think who it could be. He was Amish. She could tell that by his use of the *Deitsch* dialect. But she couldn't recognize this stranger's voice, which didn't make any sense. Seven Poplars was a small community; she knew everyone.

Heat flashed under the skin of her throat and cheeks. If she could have suddenly made herself invisible, she would have. Frantically, she drew her legs up, attempting to cover her bare shins. "I'm caught," she managed, her voice coming out in a squeak. "My dress…"

The sun was so bright that when she looked up, she could only make out the silhouette of the stranger as he leaned over her and closed his hands around her shoulders. "*Ne, maedle*, lie still."

His husky voice was rich and compassionate. She squinted in the sunshine. This was no lad, but neither did his tone have the weight and gravity of age—a young man, then. Which was even worse. She clamped her eyes shut, hoping the ground would swallow her up.

"Easy," he said. "I'm just going to—"

She felt the tension on her dress suddenly loosen.

"There you go."

At once, she tried to struggle to her feet, but she couldn't find anything solid to grab on to. Before she could protest, he had wrapped his arms around her and was lifting her out of the briars.

He cradled her against him, one arm under the backs of her knees, the other supporting her shoulders. "Best I get you to Sara and have her take a look at that knee. Might need stitches." Instead of putting her down, he turned and started to walk across the field toward Sara's.

Dorcas opened her eyes and looked into a broad, shaven face framed by shaggy butter-blond hair that hung almost to his wide shoulders. He was the most attractive man, Amish or English, she had ever laid eyes on. She parted her lips, but words wouldn't come. He was too beautiful to be real, this man with merry pewter-gray eyes and sun-tanned skin.

I must have hit the post with my head and knocked myself silly, she thought.

She was breathless again, but now it wasn't from the fall. Other than her father, she'd never been this close to a man. And this one was so large, so beautiful. And his smell. She hadn't known a man could smell so good. A small part of her brain registered the thin, patched shirt with its frayed collar, as she took more of the details in. This dream man was even more poorly dressed than her father.

"I can…I should…" She pushed against his shoulders, thinking she should walk. She could certainly walk.

"*Ne*, not on that knee. It may need stitches. If you try to walk, you could do yourself more harm." He shifted her weight. "You'll be more comfortable if you put your arms around my neck."

"I…I…" she mumbled, but she did as he said. He kept walking. She knew that this was improper, but she couldn't figure out what to do, what to say. The sun shone warm on her face; she could hear a mockingbird singing.

"You must be the little cousin Sara said was coming to help her today," he said. "I'm Gideon, her hired man. Gideon Esch. I just arrived last night from Cashton."

Little cousin? Gideon's words sifted through her tumbled thoughts. Little? She was five foot eleven, a giant compared to most of the local women, and taller than three quarters of the men in her community. She almost giggled. No one had ever called her *little* before. But what came out was only *"Vo?"* She'd never heard of Cashton.

"Wisconsin. My home." He smiled down at her, and sunlight lit his face. His eyebrows were fair and neat, his face clean-shaven. He wasn't married. Her heart pounded.

She didn't know what to say. She had to say something, didn't she? "The…stile…step broke," she managed.

"I saw. Falling into that fence. You could have been seriously hurt."

She nodded. Gulped. Maybe this was a dream…

"You don't say much, do you?" He looked down at her in his arms and grinned. "Not like my sisters, eight of them. Talk, talk, talk, all the time, until a man can't hear himself think. You know what I mean?"

Dorcas nodded again.

He grinned. "I like you, little cousin. Do you have a name?"

"Dorcas. Dorcas Coblentz."

The gray eyes narrowed, and Gideon shook his head. "You don't look like a Dorcas to me."

What was she supposed to say to *that*? She'd never thought her name suited her, either, but it had never mattered. Dorcas was the name her parents had given her at birth.

He stopped walking to look down at her with a serious face. "I don't suppose you have a middle name?"

She nodded. "Adelaide."

"Better." He grinned down at her. "Adelaide," he repeated. "Addy. That's what I'll call you. You look a lot more like an Addy than you do a Dorcas."

"Addy?" The syllables rolled off her tongue, not quite the same as the way Gideon said it with his Wisconsin *Deitsch* accent, but well enough. The idea settled over her as easily as warm maple syrup over blueberry pancakes. "Addy," she repeated, and then she found herself smiling back at him. Addy was such a pretty name.

Dorcas wasn't pretty. She had never been pretty. Her parents and grandmother had made that clear to her as a child. "Teach that one to cook," her *grossmama* had declared on the morning of her first day of school. "She's as plain of face as you were, Martha, too tall for a girl and skinny as a broom handle. And that mouth…" Her grandmother had spread her hands hopelessly. "Be firm with Dorcas while she's young, or I warn you, you'll have an old maid on your hands, just like my sister, Jezzy."

"Almost there, Addy," Gideon said, bringing her back to the present.

She opened her eyes, half expecting to find that it wasn't a handsome young man carrying her across the field, but some shriveled-up old farmer with straw in his beard and hair growing out of his ears.

But there he was. Dorcas sighed with relief, as a smile bubbled up and spilled out of her wide mouth and spread across her face. *Gideon Esch*—a perfect name for any *Plain* girl's secret wishing.

"Gideon Esch! *Was in der welt?*"

Dorcas turned her head to see Sara Yoder drop her basket of laundry at the clothesline.

She hurried toward them, apron flying. "How bad is she hurt?"

"The stile broke on the south fence line, and she fell into the hedgerow. She cut her knee on a nail, I think. She might need a tetanus shot," Gideon told Sara.

"Had one this year," Dorcas squeaked.

"I thought…it might not be *goot* for her to walk on it."

Sara looked at Dorcas then at Gideon and then back at Dorcas again. Her dark eyes narrowed, and something passed over her caramel-colored face. A thought Dorcas couldn't identify. Then Sara's eyes snapped wide and she said sternly, "Dorcas, have you lost your mind? Unless you've got broken bones protruding from that knee, you'd best get out of Gideon's arms this instant!"

Dorcas's fantasy evaporated as she realized how inappropriate this must look to her new employer. She squeezed Gideon's shoulders. "Put me down," she urged. "Now!"

He let go of her, practically dropping her, then thought the better of it and caught her before she hit the ground. Holding her under her arms, he gingerly tilted her upright.

Dorcas took a single step, winced and looked down at her leg. Below the hem of her torn, blood-stained dress, a thin trickle of blood oozed down her shin. "It's not so bad," she said.

"I think it might need stitches," Gideon protested.

Sara leaned over and carefully raised the hem of Dorcas's dress high enough to examine her knee, but not so high as to expose too much leg to Gideon. "Don't be silly," she huffed. "A little soap and water, maybe a butterfly bandage, and that knee will be as good as new." She stood up, lowering Dorcas's dress hem. "Into the house with you. Come along." She turned on her heels and started for the back door.

Dorcas hobbled after her. As they reached the porch, she glanced over her shoulder to see Gideon still standing there in his shabby, patched clothes and battered straw hat. Her cheeks burned, but beneath the flush of embarrassment, her skin still tingled with the excitement of Gideon's touch.

After supper that evening, Gideon sat in Sara's kitchen and watched as she and Ellie cleared away the dishes and put the room in order. Although he was new to Sara's, the familiar routine felt comforting. He liked this time of night at home, when supper was over and there was time to talk as the day came to an end.

The house in Wisconsin where he had grown up had always buzzed with the female chatter of a bevy of sisters, both older and younger than he was. And his mother reigned over them all. Sara reminded him of his mother in a lot of ways. She wasn't stern, but she had a commanding way about her. And she was every bit the cook his mother was. Sara Yoder set a fine table, and the bountiful meal had included a fine sage sausage and the excellent cheddar cheese one of his sisters had tucked into his suitcase. Although coming to Delaware hadn't been his choice, it appeared as though his stay might not be unpleasant, after all.

Ellie, who was a little person, had set a stool at the sink and was washing dishes while Sara dried. They were an unusual pair, and would have stood out in any group of Amish women, but both were interesting and good company. How the two had come to live together, he didn't know yet, but he had already learned that diminutive Ellie was the new schoolteacher in Seven

Poplars. The previous teacher, Sara's cousin Hannah Yoder, had recently wed and, like most Old Order Amish women, had chosen to stay at home with her husband rather than work full-time. Ellie would begin teaching in September.

Gideon's gaze shifted to Sara. He guessed she was between forty and fifty years of age. She wasn't that tall, about his mother's height, but that was where the physical resemblance ended. His mother's hair was as yellow-blond as his own, but Sara's was walnut-brown and so curly as to be almost crinkly, what he could see of it under her prayer *kapp*. Her skin was the color of his morning coffee, a chocolate with extra dollops of heavy cream. Sara was a puzzle: not black, not white, but an exotic mixture. She was unusual because most Amish were as pale as winter cream.

Ellie, in contrast, was in her early twenties, and although she was the shortest girl he'd ever known, barely four feet tall, she was quite attractive, with her neat little figure, blond hair and blue eyes. Ellie's freckled face was as fair as any of his sisters', and she was always smiling and laughing. He liked her. Not in the romantic way that a fella might like an unmarried girl, but in a brotherly way. Within the first few moments of meeting Sara and Ellie at the bus station in Dover, he had known that he and Ellie would be good friends.

Sara seemed more serious, though she certainly didn't seem unwilling to laugh. She had a take-charge attitude and a determined gleam in her dark eyes. Just the kind of woman one would expect to be a matchmaker. Though Sara was the *only* matchmaker he'd ever met.

Sara was the reason he was here in Seven Poplars, a thousand miles from home. Although he wasn't ready to settle down yet, his parents were eager for him to take a wife and start raising a household of little Esches. They'd been trying to match him up, unsuccessfully, with one local girl after another for years. Coming to Seven Poplars had been a way to escape his family's good intentions, yet he had quickly realized that it was a little bit like jumping out of the kettle into the fire.

Gideon had promised his mother and father that he would help Sara settle in to her new farm and, while he was there, let her look into finding him a suitable wife. What he hadn't told them was that just because the matchmaker might find him a girl, that didn't mean he would be willing to walk out with her.

Gideon simply wasn't certain that he was ready to marry; he still enjoyed being single too much. He loved women, young and old, tall and short, plump, thin and in between. He liked to watch them as they walked and as they sat in service, heads nodding as gracefully as swans as the preacher delivered the sermon. And he never tired of hearing female laughter. He loved escorting girls to frolics and singings, and he even enjoyed the workdays when unmarried men and women would join forces to help someone in the Amish community.

He didn't believe, as many Amish men did, that females should keep to the house and minding of children. Not at all. Having such a gaggle of sisters who helped with the family business had taught him that women could be just as clever and hardworking as men. Respect for the opposite sex Gideon possessed aplenty. What he didn't have was a desire to give up his bachelor's fun and settle down with just one *fräulein*. And he highly doubted that any eager girl that Sara could dangle in front of him would cause him to change his mind.

He was thirty years old, and his parents had been making decisions for him since he was born. He had honored them as the Bible instructed. He loved them as they loved him, as they loved his sisters. He'd always been a dutiful son. He'd studied the craft his father expected him to follow, and he'd joined the church at twenty-one, as his family had urged. Every day, he tried to live the life his family and faith inspired. But he would not marry a bride someone else thought was right for him, and he wouldn't be rushed into matrimony until he was good and ready—which, if he had his druthers, would be five, maybe even ten years in the future.

Chapter Two

"Gideon," Sara said.

He glanced up as she wiped a plate dry and put it onto the cupboard shelf. "*Ya*, Sara?" He waited, needle and thread in midair. He'd been so lost in his thoughts that he wasn't sure what he'd missed.

Sara raised one brow quizzically, and stared at him. "What are you doing with that *nodel*?"

"I was wondering the same," Ellie commented.

Gideon secured the final knot with the sewing needle and snipped off the end of the thread with small embroidery scissors.

"Just fixing the tear in Addy's dress that you had her leave here."

"I would have gotten to it," Sara said.

"I know, but it wasn't any trouble. I was able to get the blood out with peroxide, and now it's as good as new. Or nearly. I didn't even have to patch it." With satisfaction, he smoothed the lavender fabric. He wasn't ashamed of his sewing skills. They were handy for a bachelor, and he had his sisters to thank for teaching him. He could take measurements of his old shirts and trousers and make his own patterns from brown paper, too. He'd never tried making a vest or coat, but he was pretty certain he could if he needed to.

"You sew?" Sara narrowed her eyes with skepticism and came to stand beside him. "Let me see what you've done." She inspected his repair. "Amazing." She turned to Ellie. "Look at this. Such neat, little stitches. I couldn't have done better myself. I never thought to see a man with such skill. I suppose we'll have to list that on your résumé, won't we, Gideon?" She picked up a damp dish towel she'd been using and hung it over one of the chairs to dry. "So that the girls who might consider you for a husband will know your full worth. I don't suppose you wash dishes?"

Gideon grimaced. "Not unless cornered." He looked to the sink to see what was yet to be done. "Am I cornered?"

"Ne, ne." Sara chuckled. "Don't worry. Ellie and I can manage well enough without your help. I'm too particular about my kitchen to let a man help. You stick to the duties I've given you, and we'll handle the inside chores. You've enough to keep you busy outside, I'll guarantee you that. My woodpile is practically nonexistent and even in Delaware, winter will come again." Her tone became firm. "You *can* chop wood, can't you?"

Gideon grinned. "I know how to use an ax as well as a needle and thread. My father used to send me lumbering. And you know the size of the woodpile we need in Wisconsin."

Sara nodded with approval. "There's hope for you, then. But you're going to have to get girls' names right if you expect me to find you a wife. You can't go around making up nicknames for every woman you meet the way you tried with Dorcas."

"I don't make a habit of it," Gideon assured her as he smoothed the wrinkles from the lavender dress and hung it on a hanger. "But she looks a lot more like an Addy than a Dorcas to me. She's too young to be a Dorcas."

"I agree," Ellie put in. "The last Dorcas I knew was ninety, and snored through every church sermon."

"And I didn't really *change* her name," Gideon defended. "She told me that her middle name was Adelaide. I thought *Addy* fit her better." Remembering how Addy had smiled at him when he called her by that name made him smile.

Sara took a fresh tablecloth from the chest under the window and spread it over the table. "I would think that Dorcas would have a thing or two to say about what she's called," she mused.

"I think she liked it." He went into the large utility room off the kitchen and hung Addy's dress on a hook where she'd see it when she came again. Then he returned to the door-way. "If you don't need me to do anything, I think I'll go sit awhile on the porch."

"Mind if I join you?" Ellie removed her apron, then glanced at Sara. "Unless there's something else you'd like me to do?"

"Ne." Sara made shooing motions with her hands. "It's a good thing for you young people to get to know each other. Ellie has made quite a few friends since she arrived," she explained to Gideon. "She can introduce you around."

"I'd be glad to. There's a singing on Thurs-day night at the Peachys' for older singles," Ellie told him. "Charley and Miriam Byler are chaperoning. You'll like them, and they know everyone."

"You two go on outside and enjoy the evening breeze." Sara took paper and a pen from a drawer in one of the cherry side-boards she'd brought with her from Wisconsin. "I have letters to write. There's a young woman wanting to come here from Canada, the cousin of a girl I matched last year."

"Hope you have better luck with her than me," Ellie teased. She followed Gideon out onto the porch that wrapped three-quarters of the way around the Cape Cod. "I think Sara's none too happy with me being so picky with who I'll court."

"I hope she's not plotting to match the two of us up." When Gideon realized that what he'd said might offend her, her went on, quickly. "I didn't mean that you…that I thought you…" He trailed off. "I've put my foot in my mouth, haven't I?" He looked down and self-consciously rubbed the neat patch on one trouser leg knee.

Ellie chuckled. "*Ya,* you have. But don't worry. I'm not that anxious to have a match, either. I've turned down four men that Sara offered me."

"Then why are you here?"

"My parents."

He nodded, understanding perfectly. A mother and a father, no matter how loving, could be demanding.

"For now," Ellie went on, "I'm happy being single. I'm excited to teach at the Seven Poplars schoolhouse come fall."

Gideon sat down on the step and leaned back against a white post. It was solid enough, he noted, but probably needed another coat of paint. "I'm happy being single, too. It's my mother who's anxious for me to marry. And my *dat*. I'm the only son," he admitted sheepishly. "It's up to me to carry on the family name. It's a big responsibility." He frowned. "I probably shouldn't have said that, either."

Ellie boosted herself up into the porch swing and scooted back until her tiny feet stuck straight out. "I understand," she said. "And don't worry about saying what you think with me. I like it." She flashed him an impudent grin. "And I like you. You treat me like I was average-sized." She arranged her dress. "Not everyone does."

"Sometimes people feel awkward with those who are different. That kind of thing doesn't bother me. I have a cousin who's like you."

"A little person? Really?" She seemed surprised.

"*Ya*. My second cousin Abraham is a harness maker, a good one. And he's a great guy, hardworking. He married a regular-sized woman a few years ago, and they have two sons."

"Big or little, the *kinner*?"

"Average size."

"Ah. They could have been small. I think it's a worry for some. But I've never minded being short." She shrugged. "It's just who I am. God has given me good health and a good mind. Why should I complain about how tall I am?"

Gideon bent to retie a bootlace that had come loose. "If they hired you to teach school here in Seven Poplars, then your height must not matter to the community."

"I have Hannah Yoder to thank for my new position. I stayed at her house last year when visiting with Sara, and we got to know each other. When she found out that I was looking for a teaching job and had been turned down twice elsewhere, she suggested me. And..." Ellie spread both hands, palm up. "Since two of her sons-in-law are on the school board, they accepted my application. My parents thought I should come to Delaware now with Sara, rather than waiting until fall."

"Has it been hard? Moving from Wisconsin?"

"*Ya*. I miss my family, but this is a nice place. I like it here. Still, it would be nice to have a friend from Wisconsin." She uttered a small sound of amusement. "If we were friends, like a *brooder* and *schweschder*, we wouldn't have to feel awkward about being together."

"Friends." He removed his hat and pushed back his thick yellow hair as he considered it.

"*Ya*," he said. "I'd like that. And we wouldn't have to worry about Sara matching us up."

Ellie chuckled. "She could try, but it wouldn't work. As nice as you are, I'm not…" She looked at him. "Now *I'm* the one putting my foot in my mouth."

Gideon cocked his head. "You aren't attracted to me?"

She shook her head. *"Ne."*

"What's wrong with me?" he ventured, feeling a little disappointed. Girls usually liked him.

"Besides being so pleased with yourself, you're too tall," she said. "Too much of you altogether. It would give me a stiff neck to be always staring up at you."

"Right, with me being tall and you not," he answered, ignoring what she'd said about him being conceited, which he didn't agree with. Though she wasn't the first girl to ever say that, he didn't want to ruin their budding friendship by arguing with her. "I guess we'd make quite the pair, wouldn't we?"

She giggled. "*Daykli* and a *grohs beah.* Not good."

A tiny lump of dough and a huge bear. Gideon laughed. "You think I'm a bear?"

"As big as," she said. "But a nice bear. Maybe one who could learn to dance."

"Amish don't dance," he reminded her. "It goes against the *ordnung.*"

"*Voah.*" True. "But bears do not live by the *ordnung.* And if you were a bear, I think you would be one that danced."

He laughed. "Do you always get the last word, Ellie?"

"Not always," she replied saucily, "but I try. Maybe that's why even Sara can't find a husband to suit me."

Two days later, Dorcas, who was beginning to think of herself as Addy, carried a plate of scrapple, eggs and fried potatoes to her father at the breakfast table. The cut on her knee was on the mend, and she was excited that she'd be going back to work at Sara's house. She wore her second-best dress, a sensible blue one that was starting to fade from repeated washing, but was still good enough for housework, and her old blue sneakers. She'd washed and ironed the lovely green dress that Sara had loaned her to wear home after she'd made such a mess of her new lavender one. She planned to return it today.

"Danke," her father said, setting down his mug of black coffee and picking up a fork. They'd already sat together for a moment of silent grace before her *mam* had poured the coffee.

Breakfast with her parents was always a good time. Her mother was cheerful in the morning, or at least as cheerful as she permitted herself to be, and her father liked to ask about her plans for the day and tell the two of them his own.

He poured catsup over his scrapple, cut off a bite with his fork and popped it into his mouth. *"Goot,* Dorcas. You make it crunchy-brown, the way I like it."

"Enjoy it, *Dat*," she said. "This was the last of it."

"The last of all that you and your mother made?" He took a cloth napkin and carefully wiped his mouth. He was always neat when he ate, careful never to leave the table with bits of food clinging to his beard, like some men. Dorcas thought her father a very respectable man, and she couldn't help being proud of him. Of course, their faith frowned on pride. It was considered *hochmut*. But how could she not be proud of a father who was one of the two preachers in their congregation, a truly good man who lived according to the rules and thought the best of everyone?

"I saw the bishop's wife at Byler's Store yesterday," her mother said as she took the seat across from her husband. Her *mam* liked her coffee sweet, with lots of milk. Luckily, it was summer, and the milk cow gave more than they could use. She hadn't taken any of the scrapple for herself, leaving it for her husband, but he didn't know that, or he would have insisted that they share. "She told me that Sara Yoder has a new hired man. Not from around here. Up north, somewhere."

"Wisconsin," her father said as he used the pepper shaker liberally on his eggs. Two eggs, sunny side up. It was what he wanted every morning. He was a hearty eater, and he never minded what they put in front of him. He ate roast turkey breast and beef tongue with equal enthusiasm, which was a good thing, because they often had to borrow from Peter to pay Paul to keep up with the bills. "The new hired hand is from Wisconsin, same as Sara."

"If she needed the help, she could have asked one of the Beachy boys," her mother put in, sipping her coffee. She had a single egg, poached, with a slice of toast spread with honey. Rain or shine, summer or winter, so long as the hens were laying, she liked her single poached egg. And she made it herself, because she didn't trust anyone else to cook it to her liking. "Plenty of strong young men looking for work around here, without hauling one all the way from up north." Dorcas's mother glanced at her. "You didn't mention a hired hand, Dorcas. Did you see him the other day when you were there?"

Dorcas busied herself buttering her toast. "*Ya*, I saw him."

"But you never said so."

Dorcas took a big bite of toast.

"Now, Martha, don't pick at the girl. She'd taken a tumble. I'm sure her mind was on her hurt knee and that pretty new dress you got her."

Dorcas smiled gratefully at her father. She sometimes winced when he called her a girl, but this time she didn't mind. She'd told her parents about the fall she'd taken, but she had omitted the part about Gideon and his rescue of her. She hoped he and Sara wouldn't tell. It had been most inappropriate, but it had been the most exciting thing that had happened to her in years, maybe ever. She didn't want to share what she'd done with anyone, least of all her *mam* and *dat*.

"I've been wondering," Dorcas said, in an

attempt to turn the conversation to a safer subject. At least a little safer. "If you would care if I started using my middle name." She looked up cautiously at her parents.

"Adelaide?" Her mother's eyes widened in surprise. "Whatever for? You've been called Dorcas all your life and now you want—"

"What harm would it do?" her father interrupted. "It is her name."

"Exactly," she said. "I'll be thirty soon, and *Dorcas* sounds too...too *fancy*." She didn't know where that had come from and looked down quickly at her plate. It wasn't like her to fib like that.

Her mother thrust out her chin. *"Adelaide?"* she repeated. "That sounds more worldly to me than *Dorcas*. It was your *grossmama* who gave you your middle name, after her favorite grandmother."

"I...I was thinking of *Addy*," Dorcas dared. Again, she looked up quickly at her parents then back at her plate. "I think it has a nice, mature ring to it."

"Mature?" Her mother sniffed.

Her father took another sip of coffee and nodded to his wife. "Come now, Martha, what harm will it do?"

Her *mam* shrugged and sighed. "If you have your heart set on it, and your father doesn't object, do as you please. But it's a *fernhoodie* to me why you want to do such a thing. Dorcas is a *goot, Plain* name, for a *goot, plain* girl."

"I just think I'd like to go by Addy," she said lightly, not wanting her mother to know how much it suddenly mattered. Such a small thing, but the suggestion, coming from a man like Gideon, seemed right. "Addy's *plain* enough, isn't it?"

"I think it's a fine name," her father said. "So, Addy it is." He glanced at her mother. "Perfect, don't you think, Martha? For a new beginning." He patted his wife's hand.

Addy was surprised. It wasn't like her parents to show affection for each other in front of her.

"I think you should tell her," her *dat* said.

"Tell me what?"

Her *mam* pulled her hand free. Her pale cheeks flushed just a little. Addy could tell that her mother was pleased by the gesture, but she wasn't willing to show it. Some people thought that her mother and father were a poor match. Her *mam* had a sharp side and was quick, always busy, always in motion, and her *dat* was generally easygoing and slow. He could spend the better part of an hour leaning on the garden gate deciding which chore he'd start on first. And sometimes he was so busy thinking that the day got away from him. But her father was a pious man and a good preacher. Life had not been easy for him, but he'd never lost faith that the Lord would see him through.

Her mother frowned. "I didn't want to have this talk this morning, Reuben. No need to make her self-conscious. She's liable to let it go to her head and make a fool of herself in front of the matchmaker. But since you've taken the lid off the pot, you may as well serve the stew." She gestured for him to speak.

Addy looked at her father. She had no idea what they were talking about. *"Dat?"*

He shifted in his chair and cleared his throat. "Your mother and I… We thought… We've been talking about…about the fact that you're not getting any younger, and you don't seem to be able to—"

"Reuben!" Her mother rolled her eyes as she interrupted. "That's no way to put it." She turned to Addy. "We've spoken to the matchmaker about finding you a husband."

"Me?" Addy sank back into her chair. For a moment, she was stunned. "You asked Sara to… For me?" she protested. "But we don't have the money to pay a matchmaker's fee."

"Ach," her mother soothed, pushing a bite of soft egg into her mouth. "You're not to worry about the money. We'll find it somewhere. Your father can always sell off some of his beef cattle."

"Or maybe those acres of woods that Charley's been wanting to buy," her *dat* suggested.

"Ne." Addy shook her head. "I don't want

you to sacrifice what you worked all your life for. Tell Sara that we've changed our minds. Maybe if I went to visit our Ohio cousins, I could meet someone there."

"Not every girl's family pays," her mother explained. "Sometimes, it is the man or his parents who bear the expense. I've already brought that possibility up with Sara."

Addy's heart sank. Who else knew about this? Who had Sara told? Did Gideon think she was one of the girls who had to pay to find someone? How could she face him again? "Is that why Sara hired me?" she asked.

"Of course not, you silly goose." Her *mam* stood and came around the table to hug her, an act Addy found almost as startling as the fact that her parents had engaged a matchmaker without consulting her. But Addy couldn't pull away, and her mother's embrace, so rare, was all the more precious. "The new teacher helps out, but she doesn't have the strength to keep up that house. Sara needs some painting done, and help to do her canning. She'll have more girls coming to stay, and she needs someone she can count on."

"Unless you've changed your mind and you don't want to work for her. I thought you could give your mother half of your pay and keep half for yourself," her father said. "As any other unmarried daughter would do."

"*Ne, Dat,*" she assured him. "I *want* to work for Sara."

"*Goot,*" her mother said. "It's settled. You'll work and while you're at Sara's, she'll give you some instruction. You'll follow her advice and meet the men she wants you to meet. And let us worry about Sara's fee. If she makes a good match for you, you'll be in a position to help us in our old age."

Addy nodded. She had other siblings, but they were older and lived far away. It would be her duty to care for her parents when they were too old to work. It was what was expected of Amish daughters, and she would do what she could for them with a whole heart.

"Don't look so glum," her father said, wiping his mouth with a napkin. "It's time you were married, with a good husband and children of your own. My other grandchildren I never get to see. We only want what's best for you."

"Ya," her mother agreed. "I'm weary of going to my sister-in-law's family's weddings. It's time we had one of our own."

Maybe the idea of having Sara find her a match wasn't so bad. Addy did want a husband, and she was tired of serving as an attendant at her cousins' weddings. But—she sighed inwardly—who would want her, at her age? Most girls were married and had several children by thirty. No young man would want her. Sara would most likely find her an older widower, someone who already had children. She tried to imagine what such a man would look like. She wouldn't mind being a stepmother, but she hoped this bridegroom wouldn't be too old or too ill-tempered.

She wouldn't set her hopes too high. She

would do as her father always did and place her faith in God. It should have been easy. If only Gideon Esch hadn't pulled her out of a briar patch and carried her across the field like some English girl out of a paperback romance.

Chapter Three

With trepidation, Dorcas—*Addy*, she reminded herself, she was *Addy* now—approached the fence line that bordered Sara's property. The dreaded stile.

The sun was bright, and there wasn't a cloud in the sky. The day promised to be warm and humid, and she could already feel a sheen of moisture on her face and throat. She hoped she wouldn't arrive at Sara's all hot and sweaty; she wanted to appear mature and competent. Especially after last time.

But first things first—her good leather shoes that she'd left behind the tree two days ago. What if they weren't there? It hadn't rained, but the dew had been heavy the previous morning. What if they'd gotten mildew on them? Replacing the pair would be an expense that she couldn't expect her parents to pay. And she'd be mortified to show up at church in her old sneakers. She'd have to use two weeks' wages to replace the shoes, if they were ruined. And all because she hadn't wanted to put up with a blister or two.

Of course, the condition of her shoes and getting over the fence were small concerns compared to the nervousness she felt about seeing Gideon again. What must he think of her? Did he know that Sara was seeking a husband for her? Had he known before she did?

Her mother said she hadn't told her about the matchmaking agreement right away because she didn't want Addy to feel self-conscious or to make a fool of herself on her first day of work. She had done that anyway.

Addy couldn't decide whether to be pleased or annoyed that her parents had contacted the new matchmaker about her. She *did* want a husband, and she'd had no success in finding one on her own so far, but... she wished that her *mam* and *dat* had talked to her first. She might have been more careful to make a good first impression on Sara and Gideon. Not that Gideon would be interested in her—a good-looking, smart, sweet boy like him—but maybe he had a friend or a cousin who was seeking a bride. Maybe he even had an uncle whose wife had passed away, a settled man with a trade, who might be willing to make a match with a woman nearing thirty. She didn't want Gideon to think that she was immodest because she'd allowed him to carry her across the field. It hadn't been prudent, but at the time...

Addy sighed. Whatever had possessed her? She'd thought she had better sense, but he'd just taken over the situation. And she couldn't deny that she'd been thrilled by the experience. Nothing like it had ever happened to her before. Not that that was an excuse for her inappropriate behavior. She'd have to be cautious so as to not find herself in a compromising position with a boy again. Any boy. She was a respectable member of the church, and she was expected to follow the *ordnung*, which forbade certain behavior between men and women. While there might not be a concrete statement concerning girls letting boys carry them across fields, she knew full well that it wasn't acceptable.

Nearly to the stile, Addy peered behind the tree where she'd deposited her shoes. To her relief, the black leather oxfords were exactly as she'd left them. She picked them up and brushed away the spider webs. Then she lifted the dress that Sara had loaned her from her split oak basket, put the shoes on the bottom and carefully replaced the folded garment on top.

When she turned to the fence, to her surprise, she saw that the old fencing and stile were gone and the briars had been cleared away. In their place were solid new posts, shiny, five-feet-high stock wire and a sturdy set of steps with a handrail. Someone, Gideon, she supposed, had been busy.

At least twenty feet of fencing had been replaced, and there was a pile of new wooden posts waiting to be put into the ground.

Addy climbed up and over the new stile with ease and then strode purposefully across the pasture toward Sara's outbuildings. Two sorrel mules that she hadn't seen before grazed on the lush grass. The first animal paid her little attention and kept eating, but the second lifted a big head, twitched its long ears and stared curiously at her as she passed. She felt like it was staring at her—the girl who needed a matchmaker to get a husband.

Which was silly, of course. Lots of Amish girls needed the help of a matchmaker to find a good husband. There was no reason for her to feel embarrassed. Sometimes it was just a matter of fitting the right girl with the right boy. Was it her fault that she had been born *plain*, or that she'd grown so tall, taller than her *dat* and many of the men in Seven Poplars? And wouldn't it be worth it if Sara found her a good husband? She smiled to herself at the thought…a husband she could love. A husband who would love her. Love between a man and woman wasn't a subject discussed in her parents' house, but she had only to see her Yoder cousins and the fine matches they had made to know it *could* happen.

The rhythmic thud of an ax striking wood cut through her reverie. As she entered the barnyard, she looked up to see Gideon.

"Good morning, Addy," he called. He was standing at the edge of a pile of freshly split sections of logs.

Addy stood for a moment, mesmerized.

He lifted the ax to rest on his shoulder. "You're feeling better today, I hope."

"Ya," she answered. She felt her cheeks grow warm, and she fought the urge to look at the ground. "I am."

His grin lit up his handsome face, and warmth swirled in Addy's stomach. Gideon was so clean and wholesome, standing there in his worn clothes and battered hat, that she had to remind herself that he wasn't for her. It was likely his parents had sent him to Seven Poplars so that he could marry up. Hired man or not, with a strong back, an easy manner and a fair face like his, he'd be guaranteed a match with a pretty girl from a wealthy family or a plump widow with land of her own.

"Sara tells me that this is a church Sunday coming up." Gideon took off his hat and pushed his hair off his face. Moisture dotted his forehead and soaked through his shirt, revealing more of his muscular chest and shoulders than was proper.

Realizing she was staring, Addy swallowed and glanced at the ground. "At my Aunt Hannah's. Close by. You can walk."

"I'm looking forward to worshipping with your congregation."

She knew she shouldn't be standing there chatting when Sara was waiting for her, but she ventured another glance at him. "My father is one of the preachers."

"Ellie told me. She liked his last sermon, on Noah's faith."

Addy nodded. That had always been one of her favorite stories from the Old Testament. "*Dat* says that people must have thought he was crazy, Noah. To build a boat when they were so far from the sea."

"I wish I'd heard the sermon." He had the nicest eyes, she thought, so large and full of life.

"I think Bishop Atlee will preach on Sunday, or maybe Caleb. He's married to my cousin Rebecca."

Gideon sank the ax into a stump and rubbed his hands together, easing the strain of gripping the ax. "I'm looking forward to it, and to meeting your neighbors. Sara says the congregation has welcomed her."

"Oh, good, you're here," Ellie said, appearing from behind one of the outbuildings. "Addy's here, Sara!" she called toward the house. For a small girl, she had a big voice.

Sara came out of the utility room onto the porch with a basket of wet laundry. "You're early. *Goot.* Help me hang these sheets, and then we'll start painting the big bedroom. I may have girls coming in soon to stay with us while I find matches for them. It's the way I like to do things." She glanced at the wood- pile. "My, you've done a lot since breakfast."

Gideon wrenched his ax from the stump. "Best to get the heavy work done early. The day promises to be another scorcher."

"Hotter here than in Wisconsin, I imag- ine," Addy said, unwilling to walk away without saying *something* sensible.

"Ne." He shook his head. "You'd be sur- prised how hot it gets there in the summer. Unless you're near one of the lakes."

"The big difference will be in the winter. Delaware winters are mild, so they tell me." Sara held up the basket of laundry toward Addy, then set it on the porch. "If you'll take this, I'll go back for the second basket."

"I brought back your dress." Addy showed it to her in the basket on her arm. "I appre- ciate you loaning it to me."

"No need for you to return it." Sara's round face creased in a smile. "I meant it as a gift. It will hardly fit me or Ellie."

"Because…I'm so tall," Addy supplied.

Sara's smile widened. "Or we're so short. Right, Ellie?"

"*Ya*, Sara, right about that," Ellie agreed.

"But it could be hemmed," Addy suggested. The dress was so nice, but she didn't want to appear needy.

"Nonsense," Sara shot back. "The green color suits you."

"It does, Addy," Gideon added. "I thought that when you left here wearing it the other day."

Sara's dark eyes narrowed. "Gideon and Ellie seem to think you'd prefer to be called by your middle name. So which will it be? *Dorcas* or *Addy*? I need to know these things."

"Addy…I think… That is…" Addy hunched her shoulders and tried to make herself smaller. "Unless you think…*Dorcas* is better."

"I think that you can call yourself whatever pleases you, so long as it doesn't offend

your parents or your neighbors. *Addy* sounds
fine to me."

"*Ya.* And me." Self-consciously, Addy set
her basket on the porch and picked up the
laundry basket. "I'll start hanging these,"
she said. "And thank you…for the dress. It's
kind of you."

"And kind of you to come and help us get
settled. It's a good house, but it needs work."

As do I, Addy thought, *if I'm to ever have
a chance at finding a husband. I just hope
Sara is good at her job. Because finding
someone for me might be her most difficult
match yet.*

Sunday, Gideon, Sara and Ellie headed for
the Yoder farm for church services. And as
Addy had promised, her aunt's home was
near enough to walk, which he appreciated.
He'd always believed that, as much as possible, the Sabbath should be a day of rest for
the horses as well as their owners.

As they walked up the long Yoder lane,
buggies full of families passed them. Those

inside waved and called out greetings. As in his community in Wisconsin, each man was garbed in the black *mutze*, suspenders, trousers and vest, and white long-sleeved dress shirts. The men's wide-brimmed hats were black wool, similar to those worn back home. The women were in blues, greens, purple or even lavender, with white organdy *kapps*, and capes known as *halsduchs*. Children were dressed like the adults, although most boys had black straw hats.

In the Yoder barnyard, Gideon shook hands with several men. He was introduced to more people than he could keep straight, and turned to Charley Byler for help. Gideon soon learned that Charley had married one of the many Yoder girls.

"Hannah lives in the big house. She married Albert Hartman," Charley explained. "That's him over there talking to Preacher Caleb. Albert used to be a Mennonite, but he joined our church. He and Hannah live here, and my Miriam, our boy, and Miriam's sister Ruth and her husband and boys live in that house." He pointed to a small house in the distance. "Eli works at the chair shop. I farm this place. Albert is a veterinarian."

Gideon arched his brows. He'd never heard of an Amish vet.

Charley shrugged and laughed. "Long story. If Sara has any problems with her mules, she should send you for Albert straight off. He's got a real touch with livestock."

"So Albert and Hannah live in the big house, but you work the farm?" Gideon asked.

"Right. I was doing masonry full-time, but I've been lucky enough to cut my hours back so I can spend more time here, now that my family is growing. It's rich soil, a good farm, and Hannah and Albert let me make all the decisions on what to plant and what animals we raise. Other than Albert's alpacas. You'll have to take a look at them after church. He and Hannah are pretty attached to those silly creatures." He slapped Gideon on the back in an amiable gesture.

"Who knows? Maybe by the time my son's ready to take over the farm, people will be calling it the Byler place."

Gideon nodded in agreement. He liked Charley. They were close in age, and Charley seemed such a pleasant and interesting person that it was impossible not to like him. "Sara said you are chaperoning the singing coming up. I hope I'll be welcome, although I can't promise how well I can sing."

"You're more than welcome," Charley assured him. "We can always use more men. There are a lot of single young women here, if you get my meaning."

Gideon grimaced. "That should make Sara happy. Not much call for a matchmaker if you don't have girls wanting husbands."

"Or the other way around." Charley motioned toward the house. "I see Samuel and Bishop Atlee are on their way in. I think we'd best find our seats."

Several hours later, the long church service came to an end. Bishop Atlee had given a good sermon. The little man didn't raise his voice as he quoted from *Exodus*, but he didn't need to. As one, the congregation leaned forward to hear the commands that the Lord gave to Moses. So fervent was the bishop's telling of the Bible story that Gideon could almost feel the heat of the desert sun and taste the hardships of God's chosen people as they journeyed toward the Promised Land. And when the listeners rose to sing the traditional German hymns that brought the worship service to a close, Gideon joined them without reservation. He'd always loved singing, and he liked to think that he had a strong voice, even if he wasn't always quite on key.

Sitting to his left was Charley, to his right, Charley's brother-in-law, Eli. Around them were fathers, brothers, husbands and sons. The Yoder farmhouse was a spacious, two-story farmhouse with large rooms that opened through wide doors and removable partitions to join parlor, hall and sitting room. As was customary, men sat on backless benches on one side of the house, women and younger children on the other. The deacon, the two preachers and the bishop, as well as older members of the congregation, had chairs, and along the wall were several rockers for the elderly. The walls were a soft cream, the floors hardwood, the furniture sparse, and every inch was clean enough to eat off.

The song ended, and Bishop Atlee gave his closing thoughts before indicating that the congregation should kneel for a united prayer. The words were familiar and comforting to Gideon. He'd never been away from his home for any extended length of time, and he'd feared he'd feel lonely. But here, he felt instantly at ease. Even though these people were strangers, they were united by faith and common customs, and he was pleasantly surprised by how comforting that was.

He liked what he'd seen of Seven Poplars. The community was conservative but not harsh in their interpretation of the *ordnung*, and they had made his first week there a welcome one. The county was known to be good farming country, and the small Amish community seemed industrious and well-off. Houses and barns were well cared for; the livestock was sleek and healthy and the roads not too busy for horses and buggies. Gideon would be pleased to write his parents that night and tell them that he was settling in and in good health. He would not mention what he found most delightful—the abundance of rosy-cheeked young women, as fair as he'd seen anywhere.

He and Charley joined the others as they rose for the final hymn. Afterward, Charley had promised they'd enjoy a communal meal served on tables set up outside under the trees. Gideon supposed that he and the other men would carry the benches out of the house for seating. His stomach rumbled. They'd eaten nothing before service this morning, and he couldn't wait to taste whatever the women had whipped up for the meal. Like at home, he knew the women hadn't cooked today, but they'd prepared so many delicious dishes the day before that there would be plenty to eat.

After the final prayer, it took a good ten minutes for Charley and Gideon to get outside to the well where other men were washing their hands at a pitcher pump. He could see that Charley was popular. He took the time to introduce him to at least a dozen of the congregation, male and female, that Gideon hadn't met yet.

"It was a fine sermon, wasn't it, Charley?" a tall, fair-haired young woman remarked. And then to him, she said, "I'm Mary, and you must be Sara's—"

"Who else could it be?" Charley cut in and then chuckled. "This is my sister, Gideon. And yes, she's unmarried and not walking out with anybody I know of." He grinned at her. "Unless she has a secret admirer that she hasn't revealed to me yet."

"Charley!" Mary's eyes narrowed. "What will Gideon think of me?" And then she smiled at Gideon. "Pay no attention to my brother." She extended her hand and shook his, as a man might do. "I'm pleased to meet you, and I hope you like it here in Seven Poplars," she said.

He was surprised at her boldness, but not put off by it. Mary Byler was interesting, and he liked girls who were different. At home, few women would touch a man not related to them, and he wondered if the rules were different here. Mary had a firm grip and a pleasant voice. Strange that such an attractive woman was as yet unmarried by her late twenties, which was how old he guessed her to be.

"Charley has invited me to a young people's frolic," Gideon said. "Will you be there?"

"Wouldn't miss it," she said with another smile. And then she waved to two other girls. "Lilly, Violet, come meet Gideon."

Two attractive young women joined them. The first, not as tall as Mary, had curly blond hair, dark eyes and a dimple on each cheek when she smiled. "Welcome to our community," she said sweetly. "It's good to have you at our worship service."

"Gideon, this is Lilly Hershberger, one of my dearest friends." Mary indicated the second girl, a brunette with blue eyes and a pleasant face. "And this is another friend of mine, Violet Troyer."

"Violet's family just moved into our church district from Peach Orchard," Lilly explained. "That's about ten miles from here."

"You're from Wisconsin?" Violet asked, smiling up at him. "I have family there. My mother's side. The Harvey Zooks. Do you know them?"

"Ne," Gideon admitted. "I know there are some Zooks near Brushy Lake, but I don't remember meeting them."

Violet shrugged. "You couldn't forget. They're a *big* family. Especially cousin Abram. They're all big, but Abram is huge. He's over six feet tall and weighs—" She rolled her eyes. "Let's just say there's a lot more of him than there should be. My uncle wrote that Abram has won the county fair pie-eating contest six years straight. Last August, it was four entire blueberry pies."

"Four pies?" Lilly struggled to control her amusement. "That's a lot of pie."

"Charley!" A woman motioned to him. "Time to eat." She had a baby in a white bonnet and gown balanced on one hip.

"My wife and boy," Charley explained proudly.

Gideon nodded. He didn't dislike babies, but they seemed to make a lot of noise, and they all looked alike to him. "A little wood-chopper," he commented, since Charley obviously expected him to say something complimentary about the child. "Healthy?"

"*Ya*, thanks be to God," Charley answered. "My wife and me, we waited a while for him. I was starting to worry."

"For nothing," Mary told him. "The Lord chooses His own time for His blessings." She smiled again. "See you at the singing, Gideon."

"*Ya,*" Lilly agreed. "And you'd better sing, not just sit there like some of the young men do." Then the two of them giggled and hurried away, heads together in hushed talk.

As was the custom at home, the men ate at the first seating, and there was a definite hierarchy to the arrangement. The bishop, preachers, deacon and elders sat at one end of the table. Next came the senior men, then the middle-aged and younger married heads of households. As a guest, Gideon was offered a place halfway down the table, next to Charley. He knew without being told that the next time he attended church, his spot would be farther down toward the end of the table with the other single adult males. Teenage boys filled the last empty seats on the bench. Little boys, Gideon assumed, would eat at the second sitting with the women and girls.

There was a moment of silent grace, a few words from the bishop and then everyone at the table began to enjoy the food. There was little talk. Appetites were high, and it was only good manners to eat quickly, so that the second seating could have their turn. Young women moved back and forth behind the men, filling glasses and replenishing trays of bread and cold cuts. Platters and bowls were passed from diner to diner: tomatoes, green beans cooked with bacon, macaroni and potato salads, slaws, pickles, sliced ham, roasted chicken, summer sausage and roast beef.

Everything Gideon tasted was delicious, especially the raisin bread and the apple-rhubarb tarts. He wondered if this was the usual communal fare, or if Hannah Yoder and her daughters put on a special spread when they hosted Church Sunday. It wasn't uncommon in his community to just have sandwiches for Sunday dinner. Too many dinners like this, and he'd have to worry about his waistline.

"More tea?" A young woman with dark hair and bright blue eyes leaned over to fill his glass. "Did you want more ice? I can get ice."

"*Ne*, I'm fine," he assured her.

A minute later, another unmarried girl stopped to try to fill his glass *again*.

It was no wonder Sara had moved her business here to Delaware; there seemed to be plenty of available young women looking for husbands. Of course, no Amish woman wore a wedding ring, so he had to guess who was single, but he'd gotten pretty good at it. Even the shy girls had a way of letting you know that they were "in the market," so to say.

When Gideon couldn't eat another bite, he finished his tea, then waved away the blue-eyed girl who wanted to refill it, yet again. *"Danke,"* he said. "I couldn't drink another drop." She giggled and stood there just a few seconds too long before moving on to fill someone else's glass. Gideon wiped his mouth with a cloth napkin and glanced around the yard.

Children of various ages sat in the grass with books or played quietly. Several little girls had what looked like a Noah's Ark with tiny, wooden animals. Another girl, about ten or eleven, held the hand of a toddler who was dressed like Charley's son, in white bonnet and gown. It was hard to remember that he was in Delaware, a long way from his home community. Although these were unfamiliar faces, and the hat and bonnet shapes were just a bit different, these could have been his neighbors and relatives.

Gideon felt at peace. He always felt good after Sunday services, and he enjoyed meeting and talking to people. Some Englishers thought that Amish life was severe and harsh, but he'd never believed that. So long as a man believed in the Word and followed the *ordnung* of his church, he was assured of salvation. What could one ask for but faith, family and community? When he considered how much he received every day, the hard work of living apart from the world was a small sacrifice.

The bishop rose from his seat, followed quickly by the older men. Gideon stood up and left the table as teams of teenage girls cleared away the dishes and glasses for the next seating. Charley and Eli stopped to speak to their host, Albert Hartman, and Gideon decided to walk back and take a look at the alpacas that Charley had mentioned.

As he left the farmyard and strolled past the line of buggies and tethered horses, the clamor of friendly voices and laughing children faded. Earlier, Charley had indicated the smaller of two barns. A pasture with a high fence ran behind it, and sure enough, Gideon caught sight of a group of animals grazing at the far end. He started toward them when someone called his name.

"Gideon! Wait up."

He turned to see Addy walking toward him.

"I was waiting to get a chance to speak to you," she said, as she drew closer. "To thank you for mending my dress." She was, he had noticed earlier, wearing the lavender dress that he'd managed to rescue. "I thought Sara had done it, but Ellie said it was you."

She looked uncertain, and he smiled at her. "No problem. My sisters taught me. Nine of us, and me the only boy. They weren't too good at baseball, but…" He shrugged. "Not many men you know sew?"

Addy had nice hair, a soft brown with just

a little hint of auburn. She was tall for a woman. He thought he could smell honeysuckle. Was there such a thing as honeysuckle shampoo, he wondered? She wasn't what you'd call a pretty girl, but she had nice eyes and an intelligent face. Her *kapp* was spotless white and starched stiff. He knew how much work it took to make it just so. He'd watched his sisters ironing their *kapps* on many Saturday evenings and now imagined Addy standing at an ironing board, using an old-fashioned iron she heated on the woodstove.

"Not one," she said.

He suddenly realized that he'd been daydreaming. "I'm sorry?"

"Not one man that I know can sew a tear so that you can hardly see it. I don't think I could have done it so well myself. And you got the bloodstain out of the hem. Thank you. I thought the dress was ruined."

"Well, it's not," he said. For a moment, she just stood there, and the silence stretched between them, not an uncomfortable quiet, but a reassuring one. He liked that. Addy might not have the fairest face he'd ever seen, but there was just something about her... "I guess you think I'm odd that way. That I know how to sew."

"I think it's wonderful." She produced a carrot, went over to the fence and whistled. She waved the carrot, and the whole herd of alpacas trotted toward her. Carefully, she snapped the carrot into small pieces and tossed them to the eager animals.

Again, there was an easy stillness between them as he came over to stand beside her at the fence.

"I suppose you heard..." she said, breaking the silence. She grimaced. "My parents... they..." A flush spread over her face. "They asked Sara to find a husband for me."

"And you don't want them to do that?"

She dropped onto the grass, folding her long legs modestly under her skirt. "I don't know," she admitted. "It's...well, it's embarrassing...telling everyone that I need help finding someone." She tugged at a blade of grass, plucking first one and then another. "That, otherwise, I'll be an old maid peeling potatoes in my mother's kitchen when I'm sixty, with gray hairs on my chin."

He chuckled. "Sounds pretty bad when you put it that way."

She tugged at more blades of grass. "I figured you knew. Ellie does, for sure. Who knows who else does?"

"But you want to marry, don't you?"

"I suppose, but I always thought I'd find my own husband. Or..." Her eyes glistened as if she might start to cry. "Or he'd find me."

"Not everybody does it that way." He sat down beside her in the grass. "Why do you think my father and mother sent me here? I could have found work as a hired man in our community. Or I could have gone on helping my father."

"What does he do?"

"Makes sausage. Sells it to people."

"*Ach*. Sausage. Everybody likes sausage."

"And it's good sausage." He smiled at her.

"So what I'm trying to say is that you aren't alone. My *mam* and *dat* and Ellie's parents think like your mother and father. They're trying to do a good thing. Because they love us and want us to be happy."

"I suppose, but…" She tossed the grass through the fence to a young alpaca. "What if I don't like who Sara picks for me?"

"Then you say no. '*Danke*, Sara, but no.' It's easy." He grinned. "I've been doing it for years."

She turned to him with surprise. "You've turned down matches?"

"A handsome, hardworking man like me?" He winked. "I've escaped more pretty girls than you have fingers on both hands. If you think you're hard to please, I'm impossible."

"So we're both being difficult," Addy mused.

He plucked idly at the clover. "It seems that way."

"My *grossmama* says that it's pride that keeps me from finding a good marriage." She looked at him. "Do you think it is?"

"Hochmut?" He thought for a moment. "I hope not," he answered honestly. "I'd not want to think of myself as a prideful person. Hardheaded, maybe, but not full of a false sense of my own importance."

"Goot," Addy replied. "Because I wouldn't want that, either." She got to her feet and brushed off her skirts. "I have to go. My mother will wonder where I've gotten to. There's bound to be cleaning up."

He stood. "Should I come to help?"

She shook her head. "Women's work, and not so hard as to break the rules of the Sabbath. Only dishes and food to clear away."

Gideon stood there awhile, leaning on the fence after Addy left and unable to get what she'd said out of his mind. Could her grandmother be right? he wondered. Was his reluctance to choose a wife *hochmut*? He tried every day to live by the principles of his faith. Was it wrong to hope that there was someone waiting...someone he could love with all of his heart...someone special that he just hadn't found yet?

Chapter Four

Addy arrived at Sara's promptly at 8:00 a.m. Thursday morning, and by nine, she and Ellie had cleared away the breakfast dishes, picked crook-neck squash, eggplant and tomatoes from the garden, and swept the front and back porch. Now they were busily taping Sara's parlor in preparation for painting the walls and trim. The previous day, Gideon had given the ceiling two coats of a soft white and carried in two gallons of pale blue, two brushes, two rollers and a shiny new paint tray.

Addy stood on a stepladder to tape off the white ceiling molding while Ellie applied the blue tape to the floor molding. Addy never ceased to be amazed at how quickly and efficiently the little woman worked. She put Addy in mind of a honeybee, laughing or singing instead of buzzing, but constantly in motion. Any preconceived notions Addy had had about a little person had been quickly replaced with respect. Not only did Ellie do her share of the housework—Addy also found she had to scramble just to keep pace. And Ellie was always good-natured and fun to be around.

Addy had lived in Seven Poplars all her life, and it was rare that she got to spend time with another Amish girl from far off. And although, from what Ellie said, life was much the same in her home community in Wisconsin, Addy found her stories of girlfriends and rejected suitors and new jokes fascinating.

She guessed that Ellie was a few years younger than she was, but like her, past the age that most Amish girls in Seven Poplars married. She supposed that it had to be difficult for a little person, even one as pretty and personable as Ellie, to find a husband. Not that Ellie seemed to mind. According to what Sara said, Ellie was one of her most difficult girls to match, more because she was picky than because she was a little person. Addy was dying to ask how many matches Ellie had turned down, but didn't want to seem rude.

Addy slowly inched the roll of blue tape along the crown molding with one hand, smoothing it with the other. "Do you know the Zook boy Mary and Violet were talking about on Sunday? The one in Wisconsin?"

"Abram?" Ellie paused, a strip of blue tape suspended between her hands. "I don't really know him, but Sara asked my mother if she thought I'd be interested. He's a nice fellow, so I hear, a hard worker, but…" She grimaced. "Too much of him for me, my *mam* and *dat* said. Too much Abram altogether."

"He's a large man?"

"About the size of one of my father's Percheron draft horses." She giggled. "Or maybe the whole team."

"Ellie," Addy scolded, a little titillated by her new friend's daring. "That isn't kind. My *dat* says that a person is the way God made them, and we should accept them as they are."

"Ya," Ellie agreed. "But think about it. How foolish would we look together? Me little, Abram…well…Abram. If we sat on the porch swing and it didn't break, it would be like a schoolyard seesaw. He'd sit down, and my end of the swing would fly up." She chuckled and shook her head. "*Ne*, Addy. Better I be an old maid knitting baby bonnets for my sisters and mufflers for my brothers than be married to such as Abram."

"I suppose." No fat boy had ever asked to walk out with her. No boy, fat, skinny or in between, had even driven her home from a singing or a work frolic. The truth was that she'd passed her dating years watching other girls ride out with boys in their buggies, and play badminton with them on their front lawns.

Her one venture into the marriage market had been a near miss with the then-new preacher in Seven Poplars, Caleb Wittner. Her *dat* and *mam* had wanted her to marry him, and for a while, Caleb had come to several family dinners. But they'd never gotten past the considering-each-other part of dating. Caleb was a respectable enough man, but she hadn't felt as if he were someone with whom she could spend the rest of her life. He seemed a little boring to her, with nothing to talk about but his woodworking. To her parents' regret, she'd put an end to that courtship before it had even started. Which turned out to be just as well because he soon married her cousin Rebecca, and they were a perfect match.

Addy sighed. It would be nice to have someone she liked pursue her, even if she did later turn him down. But there always seemed to be more eligible young Amish women than suitors, which was why Sara's matchmaking services were in such high demand.

She climbed down the ladder, moved it over a foot and climbed up it again. The smell of baking bread wafted in from the kitchen. Sara was a fantastic baker, and she preferred to make rye or whole-wheat loaves with yeast instead of the baking powder biscuits that Addy had grown up eating. Sara liked to get her baking out of the way early in the day, and Addy's mouth watered at the thought of the midday meal they would be sitting down to in a few hours. Between the apple tarts, the *lebkuchen*, the *fastnachts*, the streusels and the shoofly pies that Sara whipped up in her kitchen, it was a wonder that she wasn't as plump as Addy's cousin Anna.

Thinking of Sara's round face brought a question to mind. Addy glanced around to see that they were alone and lowered her voice. "Why is Sara's skin darker than ours?" she asked Ellie.

Ellie shrugged. "I don't know. Don't

you have anyone with dark skin in your community?"

"Ne." Addy felt her face grow warm, and she was sorry she'd asked. Most Amish she knew were fair-skinned, with rosy cheeks and German features. Sara had curly, almost blue-black hair, but she didn't look African-American. What was her family background? *Mam* had asked her this morning if she knew.

Ellie bent over and measured out another length of tape for the windowsill. "Not so unusual to have members with darker skin in other Amish settlements. I went to school with a girl who was very brown, but she was a foster child that a family in our church adopted. Louise, her name was. Very good at arithmetic. She won the prize every year at the end-of-school picnic."

"I just wondered." Addy turned back to her task. "It's not important."

"Not all people are alike," Ellie said. "And a good thing, wouldn't you agree?"

Addy nodded, liking the way Ellie looked at things. *"Ya,* a good thing."

"What's a good thing?" Gideon came into the parlor carrying a toolbox in one hand and a door latch in the other.

"Nothing," Addy said quickly, concentrating on unrolling more tape.

Why did she always feel as if she was showing herself at her worst when Gideon popped up? She didn't want him to think of her as nosy or disapproving of the good woman who paid their wages. She'd only asked because her mother's question had made her curious.

Gideon stared at her, narrowing his gaze. "But the two of you were—"

"Is that latch for the closet door?" Ellie interrupted, thankfully coming to Addy's recue.

"*Ya*, Peanut, what else would it be?" Gideon shot back.

Addy glanced at Ellie to see if his retort or the nickname would hurt her feelings, but Ellie only laughed.

"Hard to say what you might be up to, Long Legs." Ellie winked at Addy. "All he could talk about this morning at breakfast was the Beachys' singing. Asking who might be there and if I was going. His mind was on funning and not on his plate and he salted his coffee instead of his eggs."

Gideon laughed and set down his toolbox by the closet door. "A little salt makes everything taste better, Short Stuff. And you never did tell me if you were going."

"What did I tell you, Addy? You'd think he never got away from the farm. Poor, overworked Gideon. And maybe these Delaware girls won't think you're anything special, once you're at the singing," she teased, wagging a small finger at him. "I heard you sing at church on Sunday." She crinkled up her nose. "You probably shouldn't be the loudest."

Gideon laughed and slapped his knee.

Addy pretended to concentrate on peeling back a little bit of the blue tape where she'd laid it crooked. She wondered why Gideon was so amused by everything Ellie said, even when she made jokes at his expense. She treated him like a pesky younger brother, and he seemed to love it. The thought that Gideon might be interested in Ellie gave her a hollow feeling in the pit of her stomach, and she immediately felt guilty. What if they did like each other?

Maybe Ellie's parents wouldn't care if a poor hired hand courted her. Addy didn't know how much Ellie's family was offering to entice a husband, but if there was land or a nice dowry at stake, Gideon's family might well overlook her size. Clearly, he didn't mind.

Most young men either learned a trade or farmed, but land cost so much that few boys could hope to start farming without the backing of their families. By the looks of Gideon's ill-fitting and patched clothing, he couldn't expect any financial support to buy property.

She immediately felt bad that she'd judged him, but facts were facts. A strong back and a handsome face weren't enough to get by on. Life was difficult, and she knew it. Even though her father owned a farm, times had always been tough for them. Many times, she'd seen her mother make it over, make it do or do without. Just because the Amish lived apart from the world didn't mean that they didn't have taxes to pay and expenses to meet. Her mother had urged her to take a husband who had a solid future, a man with prospects, and Addy could understand why. She hoped that if Ellie did like Gideon, she realized what she was getting into.

Or maybe the give-and-take between Ellie and Gideon was as innocently lighthearted as it seemed, and the two of them knew how to play the game that no one had ever explained to her. Maybe if she'd grown up with brothers as Ellie had, she would be more at ease with the opposite sex, but there was no changing that. Addy was what she was, and even with a pretty new name and dress, underneath she was just as awkward as ever.

"What about you, Addy?" Gideon asked. "You're going to the Beachys' tonight, aren't you?"

She pretended to concentrate on attaching the strip of tape. She didn't know what to say. Of course, she loved get-togethers with singing, good companionship, prayer and laughter. All her unmarried friends would be there. But for several years, she'd been one of the older girls, and it got harder and harder to watch other young women ride or walk home with the boys while she caught a ride with a group or walked home alone. The last time she'd attended a gathering, a taffy-pull two weeks earlier, her *dat* had let her take the horse and cart. That had been just as bad because, once again, she'd driven home alone while all the other girls seem to have paired up with young men.

Addy was beginning to feel as if she were one of the chaperones rather than one of the girls. And maybe that was what it would come to. Her last birthday was months ago, but it would come again soon enough, and when it did, she'd be thirty. The thought made her stomach turn over. Most girls married by twenty-five, and as her mother was quick to remind her, time to make a good marriage was fast running out.

"What is it with you two?" Gideon demanded. He assumed a solid stance, legs slightly apart, arms folded over his broad chest, and scowled at them. "Yes or no? Am I the only one of the three of us who wants to have some fun?"

Ellie threw up her small hands in surrender. "All right, all right," she said. "I'll go."

"Addy?" He turned those beautiful gray eyes on her, and her heart skipped a beat.

"Maybe," she managed.

He spun around to look back at Ellie. "How far away is the Beachy farm?"

"A mile and a half, maybe," she answered.

"Good, we'll walk." He swung back around. "So, it's decided. We're all going. Addy, we'll swing by your house and pick you up on our way. I may not convince any of the pretty girls to let me walk them home, but at least I'll arrive with two."

Thrilled, Addy grabbed ahold of the ladder with one hand to steady herself. Gideon

wanted her to go to the singing! He'd asked—
no—he'd *insisted* that she walk to the frolic
with him. Happiness bubbled up in her chest,
and she felt a little lightheaded. No boy had
ever insisted she go to a youth gathering before. And none had ever promised to come
by and get her. She felt that she should say
something, but she was struck speechless
with excitement. All she could do was nod.

"It's settled, then." Gideon clapped his
hands together and turned to the sagging
closet door. "We're going, and we'll have a
wonderful time. And I'll prove to you—" he
indicated a chuckling Ellie with a raise of his
chin "—that Half Pint here doesn't recognize a fine voice when she hears it."

Elmer Beachy had passed the word that
the singing at his father's home would start
at seven, but by the time Gideon, Ellie and
Addy got there, a spirited volleyball game
was already in play. The walk from Addy's
farm hadn't been that far. Instead of taking
the road, they had followed the path that led

through her Aunt Hannah's farm to the Seven
Poplars schoolhouse, where Ellie would be
teaching in the fall. Once they reached the
schoolyard, it had only been a short distance
to the Beachys' lane.

More than a dozen buggies and a few wag-
ons had passed them, but Addy had refused
the offered rides, giving the excuse that she
wanted to stretch her legs. What she'd really wanted was to prolong the time she and
Ellie spent with Gideon, talking and laughing. Addy had never felt excluded from the
life of the community, and she had certainly
always had friends. But her place had always
been on the outside of a circle, never the center. Being with Ellie and Gideon made her
feel special, even if she suspected he'd asked
her to walk with them just to be kind. They
did all work for Sara, and it would have been
rude not to invite her.

But this evening, the tables were turned.
It was Addy who knew everyone and introduced the strangers. Of course, Ellie had
been in Seven Poplars for a few weeks, but

the people she had met before were mostly from their church district. Tonight, unmarried Amish young people would gather from all over Kent County for the singing. And although their host, Elmer Beachy, had recently turned only twenty, the majority of his guests were a little older. It was a relief to Addy to know that she wouldn't be competing with sixteen-year-olds. Not that a singing was a competition, but it was one of the few social occasions where rules of behavior keeping boys and girls apart were somewhat relaxed.

Singings were wholesome fun. It was an exciting time when anything could happen. She could make a connection with a young man, and he might ask her to ride home in his buggy. It had never happened yet, but she continued to hope. She felt better about her appearance since she'd gotten her broken tooth repaired the previous year, and she knew she looked her best in her new dress.

"Gideon!" Lilly shouted as the three

approached the volleyball game. "We need another fellow!"

"Sure," he answered. He snatched off his hat, tossed it to Ellie and quickly found a place in the formation.

"You know how to play?" Mary asked, then served the ball over the net.

Thomas volleyed it back to what looked like a hole in the defense, but Gideon lunged forward, dove and sent the ball flying back to land just inside the line, scoring for his team. Lilly shrieked with joy and threw her arms in the air. "Did you see that?" she cried, clapping her hands.

"Beginner's luck!" shouted Menno from Thomas's team. "Your serve again, Mary. This time we'll be ready for you!"

Addy and Ellie sat down on one of the bales of straw set out for those waiting to take a turn playing, or who just wanted to watch.

Gideon quickly scored another point for Mary's side, and a crowd gathered to watch. "I think Mary brought in a ringer!" someone called. "Maybe those Wisconsin boys play professional!"

Thomas leaped high to block the ball, volleyed it back to Elmer, who tried to slam it down just beyond the net, but the ball caught and fell just on the far side. Someone called out the new score, and Menno groaned. Mary served a third time; the ball went back and forth, and then Elmer crashed into a girl Addy didn't know, and three of the team went down in a heap. The ball struck the ground well inside their court, giving Mary's team another point.

"I love your dress, Dorcas," Violet said, sitting down on the bale of straw between her and Ellie. "It's new, isn't it? You look good in that color. Doesn't she, Ellie?"

Ellie nodded, smiling at Addy. "*Ya*, I think so. Very nice."

"*Danke.*" Addy said. She wished that Violet hadn't called her by her old name, but she felt uncomfortable making a point of it.

Ellie spoke up. "Dorcas is using her middle name now. It's *Adelaide. Addy.* What do you think? Suits her better."

Violet considered. *"Addy."* Her pretty face broke into a smile. *"Ya,* that's better. I like it."

Violet had always been one of the popular girls, a young woman who always had boys vying to drive her home. Violet was fun to be around, always ready with a quick smile and a willing hand to help at suppers and work frolics. The two of them had never been close friends, although Violet had never been unfriendly. It warmed Addy's heart that Mary's friend had sought her out and that she approved of her new name.

Now Violet leaned close. "He's cute, isn't he? And a good player."

"Gideon?" Addy fixed her eyes on the fast-moving game. "I…I suppose." She thought she should say something more, maybe about what a hard worker he was, or the fact that he was talented with a needle and thread, but fearing she might say the wrong thing, she just concentrated on the game.

A few minutes later, there was a shout and raucous cheers as the game came to a triumphant end with Mary's team winning 15-12. Charley Byler appeared and directed the two teams to change players. Someone appointed Gideon captain of the red team, and he insisted that Thomas, Ellie, Violet and Addy play on his side. They tied up the game several times until finally the other team won by the required two points. Addy didn't mind. She had played well, and even though she hadn't scored any points, she'd kept up an adequate defense. Best of all, she'd enjoyed herself immensely.

After the game, everyone moved on to the actual singing part of the frolic and Addy's cousin Miriam made an announcement. Instead of sitting boys on one side of the long table and girls on the other, they were mixing things up.

There was a short break so that the guests could choose from iced tea, lemonade, water or soda pop before proceeding to collect their hymn books and take their places. Miriam and Charley, as chaperones, didn't sit on the singing benches but made themselves busy setting out bowls of chips, cookies and popcorn.

"Everyone line up," Charley instructed. "Now every third person trade places with the neighbor on their left." There were giggles and comments as everyone did as he asked. "Good," he declared. "Now every fourth person trade places with the second." He kept on until no one in the group was standing with any of the friends with whom they'd arrived.

One of the younger Beachy children came out with a wooden bowl. In it were homemade taffies, each wrapped in wax paper, some candies white, others black. "Everybody choose one," Charley said. "Now line up again, and find a seat on either side of the table. Don't open your candy yet. Wait until I tell you." Guests began taking their places. "Not there, Menno," Charley called. "Boy, girl, that's it."

Soon everyone was seated, if not quiet.

To her surprise, Addy found herself beside Gideon.

"Is this the way you always do things here?" Gideon whispered.

"Ne," she whispered back. Sitting as close as they were on the backless bench, it would be difficult not to accidently brush against Gideon. She sat up straight, determined not to let that happen. What would he think if her knee touched his? Or if she shifted her foot and stepped on the toe of his shoe? What was Charley thinking?

Gideon grinned at her. "I didn't say I didn't like it."

Mary was one of the lead singers, and she silenced the group by choosing the first hymn. It wasn't one of the slow, High German hymns usually sung at Sunday worship, but a faster one, more of a gospel tune. There were no instruments. Guitars, harmonicas or electronic music weren't permitted in the Seven Poplars community, but everyone was used to singing without accompaniment.

As Ellie had warned her, Gideon sang with

enthusiasm and volume, if not perfect pitch. Addy thought it charming. Who cared if he was a little off-key? Everyone was having such a good time. She doubted anyone but those sitting on either side of him even noticed.

Thomas picked the second hymn, one so familiar that no one, not even Gideon, needed the hymn book to follow the words. They sang all six stanzas and ended with applause. Then Charley said, "Why don't we let our newest arrival pick the next song? Gideon? Would you like to choose?"

"We do clapping games at home," he said. "Is there any rule against it here?"

Charley grinned and shook his head. "Not as long as you keep your hands where we can see them," he teased.

Laughter rang out around the table.

"Just remember," Charley went on, "Bishop Atlee is up there in the hayloft watching every move you make."

Again, there was laughter. No one was offended by Charley's remarks, which was one of the reasons he and Miriam made such good chaperones. Addy had been afraid that after they had their baby, they'd be too busy for young people's frolics, but so far, they'd been making the events regularly.

"All right," Gideon said. "Does everybody know 'Froggy Went a Courtin''? The tricky part is that first the boys sing the song and the girls clap and sing the chorus, and then you switch on the second stanza. First one to mess up or clap when it isn't their turn loses a point. Boys versus girls. The side that loses—that gets ten points first—has to do cleanup before we go home. Ready?"

"Just one thing," Charley said. "Before you start the song, everyone unwrap their taffy and pop it in their mouth."

"Oh," Miriam called. "I have to warn you. Some are made with sugar and some with lemon."

"Ne!" someone yelled. "No fair!"

Addy grimaced, unwrapped her candy and put it in her mouth. The sweet flavors of butter, vanilla and sugar flooded her mouth.

Gideon gave the signal and the boys began to belt out "Froggy Went A Courtin'." Laughing, Addy savored her treat, hoping that the whole evening was going to be as sweet and wonderful as her taffy.

Chapter Five

The girls won the singing game, as Gideon had expected. He could always count on one of the guys to clap or start to sing the chorus when it wasn't their turn. The defeat was declared amid a great deal of groaning on the boys' side and cheers and laughter from the girls. Since he'd picked "Froggy Went a Courtin'," he was expected to name the next lead singer—the person to choose the song—and he called on Ellie.

She suggested "She'll Be Coming 'Round the Mountain," boys to stomp and clap, and girls to add appropriate hand motions, such as "urging on the six white horses" and "chopping the head off the old red rooster." Enthusiasm rose with each chorus, and by the end of the tune, everyone was laughing so hard at others' antics that they could barely get out the words.

Charley and Miriam passed out glasses of cold iced tea, along with bowls of popcorn and potato chips. After a noisy break for refreshments, Ellie nodded at Addy to choose the next song. For a moment, Addy seemed flustered and embarrassed to be called on. Her cheeks flushed as she picked up her songbook and fumbled through it. She looked up and saw *him* watching her.

"Page…" She lost her page and blushed even redder. Someone snickered, and Addy looked ready to burst into tears.

"'Amazing Grace'?" Gideon prompted.

Addy nodded.

"'Amazing Grace,'" he repeated firmly. "I think we all know that one by heart."

The others stood, and Ellie began the hymn, although by custom, it should have been Addy leading. Addy stumbled on the

first word and then picked up a few notes
later. Gideon couldn't imagine why she was
so rattled. At Sara's, she never seemed reluctant to speak up, and her voice was amaz-
ingly good. At the end of the song, she
pointed at Thomas, who chose a fast hymn.
Two more followed before Miriam suggested
a more serious one, and when it was over,
asked for silent grace.

After the blessing of the meal, Charley
waved the group to help themselves to sandwiches, fruit and cookies. The light supper took the better part of an hour, during
which boys and girls talked freely. Gideon
was pleased to get to know Charley's sister
Mary better, along with her friends: the vi-
vacious Lilly, and another girl, Gerty, who'd
come with a group from another church
district. Gideon would have liked to have
driven any one of them home. Unfortu-
nately, he didn't have a horse or a vehicle
to take them; his only option was to offer
to walk a girl home. Being a poor hired

hand, he was learning, had serious drawbacks where dating was concerned.

When he admitted as much to his new male friends, Thomas called Menno over to the table where the boys were all gathered around plates of sandwiches. "Shouldn't be hard to figure out a way to solve your problem," Thomas said. "Titus asked Lilly to act as a go-between and see if Gerty would be willing to ride home with him. Lilly thinks Gerty might, but she won't accept if there isn't a second couple."

Gideon nodded. He could see where this was going. Customs seemed to be the same as in Wisconsin. Fellows didn't directly ask a girl to go out with him. They found a girlfriend to approach her, thus avoiding embarrassment if the object of a guy's attention wasn't interested. "Does Lilly have a date yet?" Gideon asked. Lilly was his first choice, but he'd seen several other cute girls, including Jane Stutzman, who might be possibilities. He surely hoped that he wouldn't strike out. He hadn't gone home alone from a singing since he was sixteen.

Thomas grinned. "I don't suppose you'd be interested in being half of that second couple?"

Gideon lowered his voice. "Keep talking."

"Titus has his *dat*'s buggy," Thomas explained. "You and Lilly, Titus and Gerty. Think you can convince Lilly? She doesn't know you all that well, but she's known Titus all her life."

"You'd get the better of it," Titus teased between bites of his ham sandwich. "I'd have to sit on the front seat to drive, and you and Lilly would be in the back in the dark."

"Where nobody would see if you wanted to try for a smooch," Thomas said. "Lilly lives about two miles from here. You can walk her to the house from the end of the driveway, and if you're lucky, you can sit on her front porch with her for a while. It's an easy distance back to Sara's."

"Her *dat* is strict, though," Menno cautioned. "And he has ears like a bat." He stuck his hands in his trouser pockets and leaned closer, as if he had a secret. "The last time I—"

"Don't make it sound worse than it is," Thomas interrupted, giving Menno a warning look. Then he returned his attention to Gideon. "Ignore him, Gideon. He likes Lilly. Everybody likes Lilly. She's a lot of fun, but she's a good girl. You might steal a kiss, but that's a maybe. And if her *dat* catches you, he'll report you to Samuel Mast."

"He's our deacon," Menno explained. "And he's tough."

"Tough enough," Thomas agreed. "And Menno should know. Last spring, Samuel made him chop and stack enough cordwood to last the school for three months."

"What did you do to warrant that?" Gideon asked.

"I'll never tell." Menno smirked and reached for a third sandwich. "But it was worth it. Lilly is the prettiest girl in Kent County. And she's not a bad cook. Makes a tasty strawberry pie."

"Too pretty for you," Thomas joked. "And if Lilly ever kissed you, I'll kiss one of those big mules of Sara Yoder's. Right on his slobbery lips."

Several of the other boys laughed.

"She might have kissed me," Menno countered, "if the dog hadn't started barking and her *dat* hadn't stuck his head out the window and told Lilly to come inside."

"*Ya,* Lilly *might* have kissed you," his brother Titus chimed in, joining them, "if she had been blindfolded, spun around and thought it was me she was kissing."

There was more laughter. Gideon moved away from the table, into the shadows of the barn. Thomas, Menno and Titus followed.

"The trouble is," Gideon told them quietly, "that as much as I'd like to take Lilly home and watch for shooting stars on her front porch, I walked here with Addy and Ellie."

"Addy?" Menno questioned. "Who—"

Thomas laughed. "He's talking about Dorcas. I heard her talking to Miriam. She's decided to use her middle name."

Menno tugged his straw hat off and pushed his hair back off his face. "And Martha let her do it?"

"Why not?" Gideon shrugged. "She's a little young to go by *Dorcas*."

"Not exactly young," Menno replied. "She's older than me and Titus."

"And what?" Gideon finished off the last of his sandwich. "You two are graybeards?"

"*Ne*, just most of the girls around here marry younger. Dorcas has always been kind of…"

"Kind of what?" Gideon asked, suddenly becoming serious. "I work with her. She seems like a good person to me. Not the prettiest girl, maybe, but she has nice eyes. And she's smart and hardworking."

"Takes after her mother," Thomas said. "Martha has a sharp tongue, but she's there when anyone needs help."

"So…" Gideon grimaced. "As much as I'd like to be alone with Lilly, I can't just leave the new schoolteacher and Addy to walk home alone." He glanced around to make certain no one else was close enough to hear what he was saying. "It's just not right."

"Why not?" Menno asked. "It's across the road and down the path to Dorcas's—" he corrected himself "—*Addy's* Aunt Hannah's. Then through the orchard to her *dat*'s farm. Sara's place is the next one over."

"That's not the way we do things at home," Gideon said regretfully. "So, unless..."

"Unless?" Thomas said.

"Unless I can get some help here, it's not going to work out." Gideon turned to Menno. "Didn't I see you drive here alone? In a gig?"

"Me? *Ne*, not me." Menno shook his head. "I'm not getting stuck with Dorcas...I mean, Addy," he protested.

"Why not?" Gideon asked. "I know her father's a preacher, but—"

"Not me." Menno shook his head. "You like her so much, *you* take her home."

Gideon shrugged. "Can't. I work at Sara's with her. How would that look to people? If I walked her home by herself—you said her mother was strict—her parents might make her quit at Sara's. Besides…" He grinned at Menno. "I think of her as a friend…maybe another sister."

"Corn toss!" Charley shouted. "Come on, fellows! No hiding behind the barn. This is a social. You need to team up for corn toss."

"Come on," Titus said. "You owe me."

"I don't owe you," Menno grumbled.

"What's wrong with Addy?" Gideon pressed.

"Nothing wrong with her, not really. She's just… She can be outspoken for a woman. She's not…you know…sweet?"

"Come on," Titus said to Menno. "We didn't ask you to kiss her, and you know you owe me a favor for covering for you with *Dat* when you got in late last Sunday night."

Charley called again. "Are you guys coming or not?"

"We still need to find someone for Ellie, too," Gideon reminded them.

"Not a problem," Titus assured him. "All settled. Thomas is sweet on her. She's already agreed to let him drive her back to Sara's."

"Come on, Titus," one of the other guys called. "We're waiting on you fellows."

"It's settled, then," Gideon said, grabbing Menno's hand and shaking it. "You'll see Addy home, and you'll be on your best behavior. And don't—"

"*Ya, ya,* I know," Menno grumbled. "I shouldn't call her *Dorcas.*"

"Good man," Gideon answered. He liked Thomas and his two friends, and it was nice to find other young men here in Delaware whom he could be pals with. At home, he'd been part of the same crowd of guys since they were in first grade. In Amish communities, it was customary for young people to form tight bonds with others their own age, friendships that often lasted for decades. He missed the camaraderie of his buddies almost as much as he missed his family. He'd hoped to enjoy tonight's singing, and—if he could get Lilly to go along with his plans—

it looked as though it might turn out to be even more fun than he'd expected.

As the four of them joined the rest of the group, Gideon found that Charley had again paired them up, girl-boy, girl-boy. Corn toss, which was basically a beanbag game, was a popular game at home, and he was good at it. Gideon enjoyed competitive games and was pleased to see that the Seven Poplars community wasn't too conservative to allow their youth some leeway at their singings. He knew that there were other areas where boys and girls had drinking parties. *Rumspringa*, they called it, the running-around time. But it wasn't permitted in his community. He could honestly say that he'd never tasted alcohol and never wanted to. He had too much respect for his parents and the church teachings, and for his own body. But he had to admit that Charley's unexpected suggestion of pairing boys and girls together during the singing and games was daring enough to be exciting.

As Gideon lined up to be chosen for a

team, he wondered which of the girls he'd have as a partner. He hoped it might be Lilly or even the sassy Violet.

As usual, Addy stood alone, watching as one couple after another paired up for the corn toss game. There were only three girls left: Ellie, Jane Stutzman and herself. Maybe, if Jane found a partner, she and Ellie could make a team. She was about to suggest just that to Ellie when Thomas came around the barn followed by the brothers Titus and Menno, and lastly, Gideon.

"What? Did you start without us?" Thomas teased. "Who's left?" Then he caught sight of the three of them. "I want Ellie!" he declared. She laughed good-naturedly and went to stand beside him.

Titus motioned to Jane, and she hurried over. Their parents were friends, and although the two had never dated, they knew each other well enough not to be embarrassed. That left Menno and Gideon. Addy felt herself flush. It was clear that neither of them would have picked her if they'd had a choice.

Please, Addy thought. *Let it be Gideon, not Menno. Anyone but Menno.* When they'd been in the eighth grade, she'd confided to her mother than he'd been letting other boys listen to his battery-operated radio. That had been a mistake because her *mam* had overreacted, told the deacon and Menno had been chastised in front of the whole congregation. Menno had been put out with Addy for months, and while she was sure he'd gotten over it, the two of them had never known what to say to each other. Having Menno be forced to take her as his partner would be so awkward. Unconsciously, she held her breath.

Menno looked around and took a step backward.

Could anything have been worse? Addy thought. Why didn't the ground just open up and swallow her? She should never have come. Her *mam* was right—she was too mature for youth singings. "You two partner up," she said in an effort to avoid even more embarrassment. "I don't really want to—"

"Are you sure this is fair to the rest of us?" Gideon said loudly, cutting her off midsentence as he pointed at her and then himself. He turned to Charley. "You've probably heard that I'm the corn toss champion of our county. And anyone who's ever watched Addy pitch corn to Sara's mules should be worried. With Addy and me paired up as a team, nobody else has a chance of winning."

Laughter rippled through the group.

Speechless, Addy stared at Gideon. Had he just bragged about himself? And about her? It was scandalous. No Amish boy that she'd ever known would have thought of boasting about his ability. It went against the core teachings of the faith. The common good, modesty and meekness were stressed. She hadn't thought Gideon to be proud. He must have said that just to make her feel less conscious about being the last girl chosen. If he had, it was the nicest thing any young man had ever done for her. She smiled at him gratefully.

Corn toss, softball and volleyball were some of the few sports where competition was encouraged. When she was in school, Addy had taken part in egg and spoon races, apple bobbing and sack races, but she'd never won anything. She could throw a softball fairly well, but she'd only played corn toss a few times. She wasn't sure she could score well enough to help Gideon win.

But he seemed to think she could. Either that, or he didn't care whether she could play or not. The thought was overwhelming, but then she summoned all her courage and did something almost as shocking. She sucked in a deep breath and declared, "Gideon's right. None of you will come close to our score." It was a brazen lie, but Gideon had sacrificed his reputation to protect her, and she had to support him.

She knew she'd never been popular, so it didn't matter so much. The community expected her to be prickly. But Gideon was an outsider. She didn't want them to think he had English ways or thought himself better than them. She had to speak up and give them all something else to talk about. And as soon as the bold words were out of her mouth, she frantically tried to think of some further way to defend him. But before she could, Ellie spoke up.

"Gideon's not exactly telling the truth when he says he's the *county* champion," Ellie called in a loud, clear voice. "Gideon won the corn toss competition in Cashton, Hillsboro, Medford and Clark Counties. And he was the top scorer at the Wisconsin State Fair last year. I think that makes him a state champion."

"That was Wisconsin," Thomas shouted. "Wait until you see what us Delaware boys can do."

"You tell him," Jane called good-naturedly. Others joined in the friendly teasing and the couples lined up to play.

The game was simple. Someone had set up two wooden platforms measuring two feet by four feet. The playing boards were fashioned of plywood and painted with crudely drawn corn stalks on each one. The boards were angled so that the top was about a foot off the ground and the bottom at least four inches.

Opposing teams competed by tossing beanbags filled with corn kernels into a single six-inch-round hole cut near the top of the board. A beanbag through the hole was worth three points, while one that stayed on top of the platform without sliding off onto the ground was worth one point.

Charley had marked out a pitcher's box with lime a distance from the corn boards. Each player got four chances to get their beanbags in, in each inning, and any player who stepped over the line was automatically out of the game. The first couple to make twenty-one points was the winner. Then the winning teams of the first round stepped aside to compete again against other finalists.

Addy was nervous when it came her turn

to throw, but Gideon had gone first and earned ten points. "Take your time," he cautioned. "And don't worry. We're a shoo-in."

Her first beanbag missed the hole, struck the board over the opening and lay with part of the bag hanging over the edge of the hole. Her hands were shaking when she raised the second beanbag. This time, she kept her eyes on the board and threw with a little less force. To her surprise, the bag dropped neatly through the hole.

"What did I tell you?" Gideon leaped straight in the air and laughed. "Did I tell you? She's a natural!"

Her third throw overshot the target, landed on top of her first beanbag, and teetered there. "Go in," Addy urged. "In." And then, as she stared at the beanbags, both slid into the hole and plopped onto the grass. Everyone began to cheer.

"One more, Addy. Go for it!" Gideon yelled.

Mary clapped and laughed. "You can do it, Addy!"

Addy made her final throw of the inning and shut her eyes as the beanbag left her hand. She was afraid to look, but Gideon's excited shout told her that she'd scored. Twelve points for her, plus Gideon's ten! Violet and Elmer were their opponents, and together they only made eleven points. Addy couldn't help breaking into a wide smile when Charley directed them to stand with the finalists.

The corn toss tournament continued until there were only two couples left: she and Gideon, and Thomas and Ellie. Charley had drawn a special pitching box for Ellie that was much closer to the board, but no one minded. With her height, it was only fair. Addy certainly didn't begrudge her friend any advantage she could gain. But no one had expected Ellie to be so good at the game.

In the final inning, Thomas and Gideon both scored twelve points, Ellie seven, and herself six, giving Thomas and Ellie the victory. Everyone cheered, even she and Gideon. He shook Thomas's hand and promised not to go easy on him next time, and she hugged Ellie. If Gideon was disappointed that she hadn't scored better this time, he didn't show it. And as for her, she was thrilled. They'd come in second place, and she'd never come that close to winning anything in her life.

To make things even rosier, Miriam produced prizes: coupons from a pizza place in Dover for the guys, and a lovely mixing bowl set for Ellie. "You get something, as well," Miriam said to Addy, handing her a new Bundt pan that would bake cakes with a raised pattern of daisies on the top. "Congratulations!"

The group gathered around the long table for three more fast hymns before ending the official part of the singing with the "*Loblied*" in High German. Afterward, there was a period of relaxed chatting between potential couples and exchanges of jokes and whispered secrets between girlfriends. The evening ended with a rousing clapping and marching version of "The Farmer in the Dell." Whether by choice or chance, Gideon ended up as the cheese and acted the part of the forlorn cheese to everyone's delight.

When the song came to an end, Addy found her cake pan, said her thank-yous to Miriam and the Beachys and looked around for Ellie and Gideon. She assumed that the three of them would walk home together, as they'd come. Instead, Menno suddenly appeared in front of her.

"Want to ride home in my gig?" He stuffed his hands in his pockets. "Would be easier, carrying your prize and all."

Addy stared at him. He wasn't asking her for a date, *was* he? There was a full moon, and although Charley and Elmer had lit lanterns that illuminated the area where they'd all gathered, it was too shadowy to make out Menno's face clearly. Had she heard correctly? Was Menno really asking to take her home?

The whole evening had been special. It had seemed like everyone had been so friendly. Girls had wanted to sit near her, talk to her. Sure, most of the girls wanted to ask questions about Gideon, but still… It was a little heady to feel popular for the first time in her life. And now a fellow wanted to drive her home in his cart?

It was only Menno, but… Addy hesitated.

"Please, Dor— *Addy*. I wish you would. Come with me, I mean," Menno said.

She looked at him. Why not? There wasn't anything wrong with Menno. When he was a teenager, he'd been chubby, bordering on fat, but in the past three years, he'd lost the extra pounds and shot up to five-ten or five-eleven. Long hours in his father's hay fields had given him a muscular body. His face was pleasant, nothing like Gideon's, but he was a decent-looking young man. He was clean, neat, even dapper, and his soft brown hair was thick and a little wavy. Somehow, when she wasn't looking, Menno had grown from a boy to a substantial man.

"Actually," she hedged, "I came with Ellie and—"

"Gideon," Menno finished. "I know. But

Ellie is riding home with Thomas in his buggy, and Gideon and Lilly..."

Addy didn't hear the rest of it. She looked across the barnyard and saw Gideon helping Lilly into Thomas's father's buggy. "They're both going with someone else," she said.

"Ya." Menno glanced in Gideon's direction.

Gideon waved to him.

Menno looked back at her. "And I'm asking you."

Suddenly, it was all too clear to her why Menno had asked to drive her home. Gideon had a date. Ellie had a date, and Gideon was too nice to want her to be left out. He hadn't wanted her to walk home alone so he'd either bribed or forced Menno to invite her to ride with him.

She made her decision in an instant. The old Addy—*Dorcas*—might have gotten into Menno's buggy because she would have thought that a ride home with *someone* was better than no ride home. But she didn't feel that way anymore.

"*Danke*, but *ne*," she said, making sure it didn't come out unkindly. "You should find some other girl, Menno. You and me, I don't think we'd suit. It's a nice night, anyway. I'd rather walk." And with that, she tucked her Bundt pan under her arm, drew herself up to her full height and walked away.

Chapter Six

Laughter, shouted goodbyes and a frightened horse rearing in its traces made it simple for Addy to slip away. Not wanting to be noticed, she didn't take the Beachys' farm lane to the road. Instead, she ducked under the electric fence, which was powered by solar panels and never worked, and walked through the horse pasture. The moonlight made it easy to see where she was going without being bright enough for anyone who saw her to know who she was.

Addy didn't want to be seen crossing the road, so when she reached the blacktop, she sat on a fallen pear tree holding her Bundt cake pan in her lap and watched as one horse and buggy after another rolled out of the driveway. A few vehicles carried multiple guests, but most provided transportation for dating couples. Singings and frolics were some of the few relaxed opportunities for young men and women to get acquainted away from the ever-vigilant supervision of family and church community.

Thomas's buggy was hard to miss. Although *technically* the vehicle belonged to his father, Thomas often used it for his socializing. And when he did, he added flashing blue lights to the red ones on the front and back of the buggy and outlined the fluorescent orange triangle on the back with a double row of red bulbs. Violet had told her that there were red and blue lights on the inside of the dashboard, and that he kept a battery-powered radio and a cell phone in a box under the front seat. Thomas had dated nearly every eligible girl in the county at least once in the past two or three years... except for her.

Addy had once hoped that Thomas would turn his horse up her driveway. He owned a bit of land, and he'd learned the blacksmithing trade from his father and grandfather and would be well set up to start a family one of these days. Nothing would have pleased her parents more than to have a young man like Thomas court her. But although Thomas had always been friendly, no spark had ever kindled between them.

Sitting there now, it wasn't the loss of Thomas that made a lump rise in her throat or made her eyes sting. It was the familiar laughter from the interior of the buggy, joined by the higher pitch of Lilly's giggle. Gideon and Lilly sitting closely together in the backseat, maybe even holding hands. Addy wasn't jealous. How could she be? She had no claims on Gideon. She sniffed and searched in her pocket for a tissue. A tear welled in the corner of her eye and dropped onto her cheek.

Why couldn't it be me? she wondered. *Just*

once. Why couldn't I be riding in the dark, with a boy like Gideon?

She sniffed again, fighting the weepy sadness that threatened to ruin her wonderful evening. *What's wrong with you? This was the best time you've ever had at a singing,* she reminded herself. She'd been song leader, and she'd won second prize at corn toss. She could almost say that she was one of the popular girls there tonight. She hadn't sat alone, eaten her meal alone or sat out and watched while everyone else joined in the fun. And she could truthfully say that she'd walked there with her new friends Ellie and Gideon, people that everyone liked and wanted to know better.

"I had a good time," she murmured aloud. "I did." Thomas's buggy pulled onto the road and turned right, outrageous lights flashing and blinking. "I had the best time," she said. Images from the evening played over in her mind, and she began to weep in earnest. "I did," she cried, when it was finally safe to cross the blacktop and hurry into the trees on the far side. "The best time ever...with Gideon and Ellie."

By the time she crossed her Aunt Hannah's quiet farmyard, the foolish self-pity had passed, and Addy had regained her composure and a measure of reason. The evening had been exciting. It had been far better than she'd expected. She should be grateful for what she'd been given. What would be wasn't up to her. It was God's plan. If he wanted her to have a husband and a family, he would provide one, but if it were her task to remain at home to care for her parents in their old age, then she would accept that with a good heart. She had her church, her family and a home. She would be content, and she would cease coveting what other girls might have.

When Addy opened her kitchen door, her mother rose from the kitchen table. She'd been waiting up for her. "You're late tonight," she said. "The singing didn't end at ten, like usual?"

Addy glanced at the clock on the shelf.

Eleven-fifteen. "*Ya*… I mean *ne*, it didn't. There were a lot of people. It was nice."

"Did you enjoy yourself?" Her mother embraced her, a rare show of emotion that gave Addy pleasure.

"I did." She hugged her back, and for a few seconds the two stood there, long arms wrapped stiffly around each other. "I was song leader one time."

"You picked a good hymn, I hope."

Her mother pulled away, but the warmth of her touch lingered. Her mother had never been a touchy-feely person, forever hugging and kissing cheeks and patting shoulders like her Aunt Hannah and her Yoder cousins. But Addy had never doubted her mother's love. Still, this unexpected gesture of affection was welcome, and Addy wanted to prolong the closeness between them.

"Is there buttermilk left in the refrigerator?" This was her mother's day for making butter. Some families had given up the time-consuming practice, but not her *mam*. Thursday was always butter-making day.

As a child, watching her *mam* dip the thick cream into the big glass churn and then turn the handle for what seemed forever had fascinated her. And the moment when the white cream solidified into lumps of golden butter remained a treasured memory. Of course, the butter-making didn't end there. The newly churned butter had to be turned out onto a clean cloth and the last of the liquid squeezed out of it before it was lightly salted and pressed into wooden molds. Not everyone could make butter, but her mother had a hand for it, and she had passed on the gift to her.

"There is. Have as much as you like, and pour me a half glass," her *mam* said. "I was wondering when you'd get in. It's not like you to stay up so late, what with work tomorrow. Did you get a ride home?"

Her mother's tone was light, conversational, but Addy knew what she really wanted to ask. *Did a boy drive you home? Have you been riding around in the dark with someone?*

Addy almost admitted that Menno had invited her, but that would mean explaining that she'd turned him down. And then her mother would want to know why and what was wrong with Menno. She could hear her penetrating voice reminding her that she was getting no younger and that Menno Swartzentruber was a decent young man from a good family, and she was in no position to be as picky as her Yoder cousins. So Addy held her own countenance and chose the easier path. "I could have gotten a ride with someone, but it was such a pleasant night, I decided to walk. Not many clouds. It's nearly as bright as day out there."

"I suppose that when I was thirty, I'd rather walk than ride," *Mam* conceded.

"Not thirty yet." Addy didn't let the hurt show in her voice.

"Not yet, but soon enough. Pray that Sara is as good as she claims, and that she can find you a husband. I just hope it wasn't a mistake to turn down Preacher Caleb. There's more to a man than a handsome face."

"I didn't turn Caleb down because of the scars on his face," Addy said softly. And that was *mostly* true. "He just wasn't right for me."

"Time will tell, Dorcas. Time will tell, and you're the one to live with your decision. I only hope you don't live to regret it."

"Addy, *Mam*. I like to be called Addy."

Her mother made a small sound that might have been amusement or derision or might have been no such thing at all. "Time for us both to be in our beds, daughter. Don't forget your prayers."

"*Ne, Mam*. I won't." Addy smiled at her mother. Pushing thirty, and her mother still reminded her to brush her teeth and say her prayers every night.

Her mother rose and carried her empty glass to the sink. The unwashed supper dishes and a few pots were already piled there, waiting for morning. Addy would rise a little earlier and have them done and put away before her parents got up.

"God keep you safe, child," *Mam* said. "And don't forget to brush your teeth."

The following morning, Addy made certain that she was in Sara's kitchen before her normal time to start her day's chores. She didn't want Sara to think the previous night's frolic would affect her work. The fact that Addy had lain awake for hours reliving the exciting moments of the evening and hadn't had more than four or five hours' sleep couldn't be an excuse for laziness. She turned away from Sara to hide a yawn. The thought that maybe she'd been foolish to turn down Menno's offer to ride home with him crossed her mind. What if she'd misjudged him? What if Menno really wanted to be with her, and she'd rejected him out of false pride? Why had she not considered that last night?

No wonder she was an old maid. The sensible thing would have been to accept and wait to see if an attraction did rise between them. But the sensible solution, it seemed, always came to her as an afterthought.

"Coffee, Addy?" Ellie asked. "Sara made bran muffins with raisins this morning. Would you like one?"

"Just coffee," Addy replied. She'd already had two cups at home, but this morning she thought she needed the extra energy. When her alarm had gone off, she'd wanted nothing more than to turn over, pull the pillow over her head and go back to sleep. "*Mam* sent you this." She handed Sara a wax-paper-wrapped rectangle of golden butter with a clover-leaf pattern pressed into the side.

"Perfect," Sara said. "Your mother has a touch for sweet butter. Tell her I appreciate it, and you be certain to take home a half dozen of these bran muffins when you leave."

She waved Addy to join the two of them at the breakfast table and proceeded to tell them what she wanted done in the house that day. There was no sign of Gideon, but his big coffee mug standing in the sink and the breakfast dishes waiting to be washed told

Addy that he'd already eaten and had already started his workday. Just as well, she thought. He would be spilling over with talk of how much fun he and Lilly had last night, and she was in no mood to hear it.

An hour later, Addy wrung out her sponge, dropped it back into a bucket and got to her feet. She'd just finished scrubbing the last corner of the room. Not that the floors had been dirty to begin with, to her way of thinking, but Sara scrubbed them every morning except the Sabbath, starting with the utility room, then the big kitchen and dining room. Rubbing the small of her back absently, Addy gazed back over the expanse of sparkling green-and-white tile with pleasure. "Well, that's done," she declared.

"My turn, tomorrow." Ellie was perched on a stool by the sink, polishing silverware. She held up a fork. "Thankfully, *this* isn't a chore that has to be done daily."

Addy picked up the bucket. To keep from walking on the wet floor, she'd have to carry the dirty water out the front door. It would have made more sense to her to begin in the dining room and end with the utility room, but Sara was her employer, and Addy would do what she was asked. "I've never polished silver," she said. "Never knew anyone in our community who had it." She'd heard Ellie say that the set was sterling, which must be terribly expensive. She'd not mention it to her own mother, who'd have a word or two to say about a *Plain* woman possessing such fancy knives, forks and spoons. Privately, Addy thought them pretty, with their swirls-and-hearts pattern.

"Me, either, not until I met Sara," Ellie confided. "She told me that the set came from her great-grandmother, and it would be a disgrace to sell it or give it away because it is beautiful."

"Is Sara rich?" Addy asked, her bucket of dirty water in her hand. She felt safe in pumping her friend about Sara because she was out in the garden cutting flowers. "My mother says that Sara is a wealthy widow who's outlived three husbands."

"Why do you ask? Are you a person who cares how much money another possesses?"

Addy was so surprised to see Gideon fill the utility room doorway that she nearly dropped her bucket. How could such a big man move so silently? She hadn't heard the door squeak or so much as a footstep. *"Ne,"* she protested a little too vehemently. A wave of embarrassment washed over her skin, and she felt her cheeks grow warm. She shouldn't have asked about Sara, but Gideon was just as wrong by sneaking up and listening in on a private conversation. "I'm not a greedy person," she added, "and neither am I so thoughtless that I'd walk on a clean-scrubbed floor in dirty farm boots." She pointed at the floor.

Gideon looked down. "Sorry, I didn't think—"

"Ne," Addy retorted. "You didn't think because you're not the one who has to mop it again."

"I'm sure Gideon didn't mean it," Ellie chimed in.

"Didn't say he did," Addy said. "Probably had his mind on last night's fun."

"There's two of us to blame." Sara appeared behind Gideon, with an armful of flowers. "But there's no harm done. This floor is already dry. A quick sweep will make all well."

Addy suddenly felt uncomfortable. Had Sara heard her question to Ellie? Would Sara think she was a busybody? Flustered, Addy backed out of the dining room. "I'll dump this bucket," she stammered. "Outside. On the lawn."

"Backyard," Sara suggested. And then to Gideon, she said, "Best you take off those clodhoppers and leave them outside on the porch. The kitchen floor is still damp. You can..."

Whatever else Sara said was lost as Addy retreated into the front hall and outside. She felt awful, and she was more than a little irritated by Gideon's remark. To ask her if she cared about money was rude. And him pretending to be so good-natured all the time. What was it *Grossmama* always said? *Sooner or later, even a black cat will show his true colors.*

She walked around the house, dumped the bucket at the edge of the field where the water would cause no trouble and then rinsed it out at the faucet at the base of the windmill. She was already beginning to regret her sharp words to Gideon. Yes, it was true that he'd tracked dirt onto her clean floor, but that was a man for you. And he had said he was sorry. If only he hadn't overheard her conversation with Ellie. She'd meant no harm in asking about Sara. After all, Sara was a distant relative, and it was natural to be curious. Addy certainly didn't blame Sara for the unfortunate loss of her husbands. What was the wonder was that Sara could bear so much sorrow and still face the world so cheerfully.

Gideon had caused the trouble. It was only common courtesy for a person to let others know when they walked into a house. And creeping up on her and Ellie and then commenting on a private conversation wasn't right. Gideon should be ashamed of himself. What really stung was his remark about her liking money. It was so untrue. The very idea of idolizing wealth went against the teachings of the church. Was he accusing her of being greedy?

"Addy?"

She snapped her head around to see Sara standing a few yards away. "I'm coming. I was just rinsing out the—"

"Leave the bucket," Sara told her. "Walk with me to the garden. I need to thin the green beans I planted two weeks ago. You can help."

Addy set down the bucket and dried her hands on the work apron. Why did she feel like a schoolgirl about to be chastised by the teacher? She followed Sara across the yard, not speaking until they reached the garden. "Maybe I was too sharp with Gideon," she offered hesitantly.

"Perhaps you were." Sara paused with her hand on the garden gate and looked into her face. "I've noticed that you sometimes have a sharp tongue, and it troubles me, because I'm sure you have a good heart and don't wish to hurt others."

Addy pressed her lips tightly together. Sara wasn't the first person to say such a thing about her—both the tartness of her nature and the belief that she meant no harm. Her own mother was quick to find fault, and Addy had often been the object of that criticism. The thought that she was following in her mother's footsteps stunned her. "I suppose I am too direct."

"It isn't my wish to bring you pain," Sara continued, fixing her with those penetrating black eyes that made Addy's stomach go queasy. "I only mention it because I share the same fault. It is my way to speak as I find, and sometimes people are less than pleased with me."

Addy stared at the grass in front of her left shoe. Had Sara heard what she'd said to Ellie? She wanted to tell her employer that Gideon had hurt her feelings, as well, but it was best just to keep still and wait for Sara's displeasure with her to pass.

"Your mother and father asked me to find a good match for you." Sara smiled at her. "I take that duty seriously, and I think that you would like a good husband. Is that true?"

Addy nodded. What Amish girl didn't hope for a marriage and her own home? She wanted children, and without a husband there could be no babies and no grandchildren for her mother to bounce on her knee. Did she dare tell the matchmaker that she dreamed of a good man who would show affection for her? One that she could learn to love? Or should she say that she hoped for a man not too old or too sour in disposition?

A dozen things came to her head to say to Sara, but most seemed ungrateful or selfish. Hadn't her own mother said that she must have a man of material means, someone who could help to care for her parents in their old age? Wasn't it her duty to keep *Mam* and *Dat*'s needs above her own? Maybe she had been hasty in turning down scarred Preacher

Caleb. He'd been a widower, but not old, and if she'd married Caleb, she'd not have to leave her family and go to some far-off community where she would be a stranger.

"Do you want me to tell Gideon that I'm sorry?" Addy murmured. The words might choke in her throat, but if Sara insisted... She didn't want to lose her job. What would her mother say to that? If Sara wouldn't have her as a helper in her house, she'd certainly never risk her reputation as a matchmaker by trying but failing to find her a husband. What a mess. And all because Gideon had been listening in corners, when he should have been in the field working.

"You're not a child," Sara said, pushing the gate wide and beckoning to her to follow her into the garden. "It's not for me to put words in your mouth. Only you know whether what you said to Gideon was deserved."

"Men are often careless about how a house looks," Addy said. "So says my mother. Even my father doesn't always think to scrape off his shoes before he comes into the house.

And when his mind is on the sermon he will give on Sunday, he leaves doors open and forgets to come in on time for meals."

Sara laughed. "Husbands. Who should know husbands better than me, who had three? All dead and gone to a better place. All faithful to the church and to our community, but all men, just the same. You think I haven't had cause to find fault now and then with their actions?" She chuckled again as she dropped to her knees beside a row of curled green shoots pushing up from the rich earth. "Start there and work toward me so that we can talk." Sara waved to a spot about ten feet down the row of green beans. "Leave about so much space—" she used her thumb and forefinger to show about four inches "—between the beans. Otherwise, the plants will be too close together and choke each other."

Addy nodded. She'd been working in her mother's garden and thinning vegetables since she was four or five years old. She knew how far apart green beans should be, but again, she'd show proper respect for Sara, who was her elder and her employer.

"I'm not one who believes that a man is always right," Sara continued. "Not even a husband or, in your father's case, a preacher. But there are ways to speak to people. And the same rule holds for women and children. If you speak too sharply, like as not, the other person is offended and either snaps back or says nothing and goes away thinking the worst of you."

"So I should have just let Gideon muddy the floor?"

Sara plucked a plant and dropped it into a pile. "Some toss these seedlings aside, but I'll sort through them and replant them at the end of the row. A few will wither, but most will slowly recover, sink deeper roots, and make a fine crop of late beans for my table."

Addy waited for Sara to answer her question, but she went on talking about green beans, about different kinds of beans, how long they took to mature and what kinds could continue to produce when the summer heat grew more intense.

"Plants are a lot like children, I've always thought," Sara mused.

"Do you have children?" Addy asked, thinking that was a safe subject and might get her past the notion of her own inadequacies.

"Dozens."

"Dozens?" Addy looked at her in surprise. Her mother hadn't been certain. She'd thought Sara had mentioned several daughters. But dozens? How old could she have been when she married the first time?

"It has never been the Lord's will that I give birth to a child," Sara said softly, "although I spent many an hour on my knees praying for one. Yet two of my husbands brought children to our marriage, all good girls and boys. And, in my years as a matchmaker, I have been blessed with helping many young men and women. In a way, all of them have become my children."

Addy nodded, sorry to know that Sara was

barren and that she had thoughtlessly asked another question that might bring regret.

"I think it was part of His plan for me," Sara explained. They were only two arms' lengths from each other now. "Now we move farther down the row," she said. "You here, and I'll start there."

Addy dropped the bean plants into Sara's hand and continued down the row.

"I was fortunate in my husbands and in my marriages," Sara went on. "Some more than others, but that's the nature of things. Maybe I could have been wiser the first time around. As I said, I was born with the same fault as you. A quick temper and a prickly disposition."

"Do you think I have a prickly disposition?" Addy's face warmed as she stopped thinning the beans and glanced at Sara. Why did Sara want her working for her if she found so many faults in her?

She bent over the beans, the color of her dark skin blending with the rich garden soil. "You're intelligent, strong, not lazy, and devout, so far as I can see. Yet you are bearing down on thirty and yet unmarried." She shrugged. "Either the young bachelors in Delaware are sadly deficient, or there is something you have yet to learn in finding the right husband."

"Maybe I'm just picky," Addy said, and then admitted what she truly feared. "Or maybe it's because I'm too tall, too plain and as skinny as a beanpole."

Sara scoffed. "Nonsense. Look at me. Short, brown as a wren and round as a barrel. And I've exchanged vows three times, each with a match who owned better livestock and broader fields than the one before."

"How can you say that, when boys flock around the pretty girls like bees to honey?"

Sara shook her head again. "A man may be attracted by a pretty face or a shapely figure, but he doesn't choose a wife for those things. A man chooses a woman who makes him feel better about himself. Who can help him be a better person. At least, it has been my experience with Amish men, who seem to me to be most sensible when it comes to marriage. A woman's challenge is to present herself as an appropriate candidate. Not a scold or a wet blanket that will hang around a man's neck and drip cold water down the back of his shirt on a winter day. I lost two suitors that I greatly favored until I learned that lesson." She shook her head. "I fear, Addy Coblentz, that I have always been a slow learner."

"And you think that if I am more careful about the way I speak to men, you might find someone for me?"

"It is my job to make strong matches, matches where both husband and wife are happy together. I've always prided myself on taking on the most difficult cases, but I've never failed yet. And I have no intention of allowing you to be the first. What would it do for my reputation if I couldn't find someone worthy for my own cousin's daughter?"

"I had an offer of marriage once…at least, almost an offer," Addy said. "But I rejected him, and he married someone else. What if I don't like the man you find for me? What then?"

"Then I'll find another. And another, until you are satisfied. Have a little faith in me and listen to what I try to teach you. You'll make some man a fine wife. All you have to do is bend a little." She held up a bean seedling. "See how they uncurl as they break through the surface of the ground? Then they stretch toward the sun, stretch their arms toward heaven and accept His blessings."

Chapter Seven

Tuesday morning, Gideon threw open Sara's back door and stood aside to let in a very wet Addy Coblentz. Beyond the porch, in the farmyard, a horse and buggy moved slowly away through the pouring rain.

"I know I'm late." Addy shrugged off her wet jacket and removed her black bonnet. "*Dat* insisted on driving me over, and he was working on a sermon." She spread her hands helplessly. "I guess the time got away from him. Sara will think I'm a slugabed—"

Ellie entered the utility room to take Addy's soggy coat.

"I should hang that outside on the porch,"

Addy protested. "It'll drip all over the floor in here."

Ellie frowned. "But will it dry out there? I think not." She gave Gideon an amused glance. "This one insisted on firing up the woodstove this morning. I'll hang your jacket on the hook behind the stove, and it will be dry by this afternoon."

"The woodstove in June?" Addy remarked.

"Gas is handy, but a woodstove gives food the best flavor," he said.

Addy stood in the center of the utility room with her bonnet in her hand and a puzzled expression on her face. Gideon noticed that she was wearing her prayer *kapp* this morning instead of her usual workday headscarf. She had on a green dress, the skirt streaked with rain.

"Is Sara here?" Addy asked, glancing around.

"Gone out." Ellie headed for the kitchen.

"On a day like this? Surely, she didn't take the buggy?"

"Ne," Gideon explained. "She's hired a

driver and gone off to Wilmington to the train station."

"She's to pick up a new boarder," Ellie explained, stopping in the doorway. "Her word for her *candidates*. This one's name is Joseph. Sara invited him to come, but didn't know he was arriving so soon. That Irwin Beachy that lives with your Aunt Hannah came over with a message yesterday. Joseph called the chair shop where Irwin works, and Irwin passed on the message. Sara must have given Joseph that number." Ellie wrinkled her small, freckled nose. "Hope she's not intending him for me."

"I thought that's why you were here," Gideon teased. "To find a husband."

"*Ya*, but I'm in no hurry. I haven't even started teaching at the school yet."

Addy's lips parted, as if she were going to say something, but then she pinched them together and looked uncomfortable. "Will Joseph be staying long?"

"Until Sara finds him a wife, I suppose," Gideon said. "I think she has someone in mind, so it may not be long." He caught a whiff of burning sausage and slipped past Ellie and into the kitchen. "Oh, no. I already burned one batch this morning."

The two girls followed him into the kitchen. He rushed over to the woodstove, grabbed the smoking frying pan and slid it off the hottest section of the cook surface. "Ouch!" He let go of the handle and went to the sink to run cold water over his hand.

He hoped the sausage patties weren't too burned to get a good taste of them. He'd used extra sage and garlic, and thrown in a measure of dried thyme, as well as red pepper flakes. He was experimenting with different recipes. His *dat* had three recipes that he favored, but the only way to find something new was to try something new. "I want you two to taste this batch," he said with as much enthusiasm as he could muster. If he pretended that he'd meant to cook the sausage well-done, maybe they wouldn't notice the black parts on the bottom.

"Not me." Ellie hung the jacket behind the

stove. Then to Addy she said, "I've been eating sausage since seven this morning. Sausage with chopped onion and garlic, sausage with fresh rosemary and sausage with sage and basil. Another bite of sausage and I'll oink like a piglet." She laughed merrily. "I'm back to my sewing. You'll have to be Gideon's official sausage taster."

"Coward," he teased Ellie. He was getting a blister on his thumb, but what could you do? Great recipes didn't come without effort, and scorched fingers were as good as sweat. "Come on, Addy." He flashed her what he hoped was his most charming smile. "You'll help me out, won't you?"

Addy was staring wide-eyed at the kitchen.

He couldn't figure out what she was staring at. Surely, she'd made sausage before. Sara had all the tools he needed: good knives, a hand-grinder, bowls, cast-iron frying pans. He'd bought the meat from a neighbor down the road. The pork shoulder was lean, and the smaller choice bits from here and there on the pig weren't too fatty. He'd had Sara pick up the spices at Byler's store last time she was there.

"I've had my breakfast," Addy hedged. Frown lines appeared on her forehead. "When will Sara be back?"

"She said not to expect her before late afternoon," he answered.

"A good thing." She was gazing at the meat grinder on the table that he hadn't gotten around to washing out yet, the cast-iron frying pans on the stove, the bowls of ground meat and the containers of seasoning on the table, some of which may have spilled…just a little.

All right, he conceded, there *was* a pile of dirty utensils and dishes in the sink, and a scale was standing on the counter. You couldn't make decent sausage if you didn't measure your ingredients by weight. Some people just eyeballed their sage, salt and pepper, but when you were careless, you never knew what you would get. And if you turned out a special batch, how could you ever expect to duplicate it?

Making good sausage, sausage that went fine with breakfast but could also make a respectable showing at dinner, or be stuffed into a goose or turkey, was an art. Not everybody was cut out for it. His *dat*'s recipes had been handed down from generation to generation for more than a hundred years, and his father thought that he ought to be satisfied to keep to what worked, but it wasn't Gideon's way. He always had it in his mind to try something different. He wanted to make a sausage that people would be pleased to share with their friends and relatives, used in a recipe that might be printed in *The Budget*. If that was pride, he was more than guilty of it.

"This kitchen looks like it exploded," Addy ventured hesitantly. "You made all this mess just from making sausage?"

Ellie giggled again and made a hasty retreat. "Sewing," she called over her shoulder as she left the kitchen. "Enjoy your sausage, Addy!"

"Sara will have your head in a bucket if

she sees this," Addy told him. She pulled out a chair, regarded the seat with disgust and went to a kitchen drawer to retrieve a clean dish towel with red roosters printed on it.

"You want bread or a biscuit with your sausage?" he asked, trying not to be hurt that she'd criticized his kitchen manners. He wanted to explain that he had every intention of cleaning it up before Sara got back. Hadn't Sara told him to do as he liked? Even told him where to find her grinder and the freshest spices in the pantry? Could you make custard pie without cracking a mess of eggs? How was a man supposed to concentrate on creating a superior sausage recipe if he stopped what he was doing every two minutes to sweep the floor, scrub the countertops and wash up his equipment?

"Just the sausage." Addy's eyes narrowed suspiciously. She sniffed the air, letting him know that she was all too aware that he'd nearly burned the sausage beyond saving.

From the expression on her face, you'd think she'd been asked to taste muskrat stew.

That was Addy for you. She didn't give a man an inch of wiggle room. To his way of thinking, she was far too critical for a young woman. And she didn't hesitate to voice her opinion. And maybe that was why he wanted to hear what she thought. Everything he'd learned had been from watching his mother, father and sisters. He was no cake baker, and his bread was only passable, but sausage he could make.

He watched her wipe off the chair before she sat down.

If he was just striving for *acceptable*, Gideon wouldn't have had the least concern. Even a little overcooked, this new batch of sausage was a good one. But he wanted better than good. He wanted a recipe that would make his father slap his thigh and nod with pleasure. He wanted to make a sausage that his grandchildren would be proud to serve their neighbors.

"Be honest with me," he said as he slid a patty onto a flowered saucer and carried it to Addy.

"What? You don't think I was honest?" Ellie called from the next room. "I said it was good, didn't I?"

Gideon rolled his eyes. "You know how Ellie is," he said in a low voice to Addy. "She's so easygoing. 'Really tasty, Gideon. This is the best one yet.'" He sighed. "But she said that even when I mixed up the samples and gave her the same one twice."

"I heard that," Ellie called.

He leaned closer. "Ignore her, Addy. Just taste it. Please."

"Do I get a fork? Or do you want me to just pick it up with my fingers?"

"Women." He went back to the cabinet, located the knife-and-fork drawer and took a fork to Addy. Then he folded his arms over his chest and waited.

"Were you really hungry, or did you just get up this morning and decide to make three pounds of sausage?" she asked.

She still hadn't tasted the sausage. She was stalling.

"Addy—" he began.

Then she cut off a piece with the side of her fork and brought it to her lips.

She was going to say it was awful. He knew it. He'd wanted an honest opinion, and he wasn't about to get it, because she was as stubborn as a setting hen. Addy had already made up her mind that because he was a man, he didn't know the first thing about cooking.

She took a bite and slowly chewed. He turned back to the stove, took out another section, wrapped it in a slice of Sara's yeast bread and ate it.

Addy didn't say a word.

He finished his sandwich and wiped his hands on a towel.

Why had he even asked her? Ellie had said she liked it. He should have waited for Sara. "Just come out with it, Addy," he said, unconsciously straightening his shoulders. He could take it. He'd just keep trying. He knew that if he put his mind to it, he'd come up with something special.

"I like the bite," Addy said, looking right

at him. "Just the right amount of red pepper flakes. And I like the amount of sage you used. Not too much. Too many people use too much. What else is that I taste?" She hesitated. "Thyme?"

Gideon could hardly contain his satisfaction. He turned back to her with a big smile. "You...like it?"

She nodded. "Really good, but..."

He leaned toward her. "But?"

"Maybe a little sugar? I could take or leave the garlic, but the onion definitely works." She held out the plate. "Let me try another piece."

"*Dat* puts a lot of onion in his one recipe, but I was trying for something a little different...something that..."

"That makes you hungry for more," she supplied.

He stabbed another piece with a fork and put it on her plate. "Exactly!"

She took another bite, chewing slowly. "There's something else I'm tasting. Something I can't quite—" She smiled at him, and her eyes sparkled. "Mustard seed?"

Gideon nodded and grinned back at her. "You've got a talent for being able to taste the different ingredients. Not many people do. You must be an excellent cook."

She grimaced and shook her head. "Not really. *Mam* says I don't have the patience for it."

He shrugged. "It's been my experience that most people who point out a lack of patience in someone else don't have much of it themselves."

Addy chuckled. "Best not let my mother hear you say that." She glanced at the overflowing table. A large pottery bowl held the remains of some ground pork. "You really made more than one batch this morning?"

"This is the third."

"Were you going to make more?" As she rose from the table, she looked at the ground pork. "You shouldn't leave it unrefrigerated. It doesn't do to leave meat out in a warm kitchen, not if you don't want to poison the bishop."

He laughed. "Haven't done that yet."

"Good for you. I nearly did in a preacher. He was coming by our house to…" Her cheeks took on a rosy hue. "Visit the family," she added, a little too quickly. "*Mam* had insisted I make hasenpfeffer because he—" She pushed up her sleeves, stepped to the sink and began to run water.

"Go on," he urged. "Why did she want you to make kidney pie?"

"Because he'd mentioned he was fond of it." She went on, her voice a little smoother. Her back to him, she added dish detergent and began to wash a frying pan. "But I never made it before, and I used all vinegar instead of half vinegar and half water and—"

"*Shtobba!*"

"Stop what?" Addy turned back to face him, hands dripping water down the front of her apron.

He folded his arms over his chest. Had he spoken too firmly? He didn't want to hurt her feelings, but neither would he be managed by another woman. He'd had enough of that with his mother and eight sisters. "Stop washing the frying pan. It isn't for you to clean up after me. I'll do that."

"When?" Her mouth was pursed in what he'd come to realize was her stubborn mindset. "You should clean up as you go. It's the only way to keep a kitchen clean. Wash up as you—"

"*Ne*. It is not the only way."

They stood there looking at each other for a second.

Addy was hardheaded; he already knew that. But so was he. "Cleaning up as you go is *your* way, Addy, not mine. And who am I to stand back and let you take on extra labor to clean up after me? In my own good time, I'll set Sara's kitchen to rights."

"There's no need to shout at me. I was only trying to help." Little red strawberries bloomed on her cheeks.

She blushed a lot. Instantly, he felt contrite. His intention wasn't to bully her. "I'm sorry.

I didn't mean to shout. But how else am I to stop you? Once a woman starts cleaning, she puts her whole mind and body into it. My *mam* and sisters once started scrubbing woodwork for a church service at our house and worked through dinner and past the supper hour without stopping. My father and I had to make an evening meal of bread and cheese and pickles."

The hint of a smile passed over Addy's features. She had a nice smile. He decided that she should smile more often.

She folded her arms and raised her chin. "Was it so terrible that you miss a big dinner?" she asked. "You hardly look as though you've missed many meals."

"It was awful," he said in an exaggerated tone. "I barely made it until morning. And that was a day of worship. No cooking on the Lord's Day. No hot breakfast." He gave her his most pitiful look. "Nothing but cold biscuits and warm milk from the cow."

"What? No sausage?" Her lips twitched.

It was working. She would forgive him if he continued to charm her.

"*Ne*. My sisters had eaten the last of the cooked sausage the evening before." He pressed his advantage. "The morning service was a long one. The preachers didn't finish the last sermon until long after the sun was high."

"Milk and biscuits is all your *mam* fed you? No jam on the biscuits? No honey? No applesauce or canned peaches?"

He shook his head. "*Ne*. Well…apple butter. Just a smidgen. And a little cheese."

"And what else?"

He grinned at her. "A big ol' hunk of pumpkin pie."

Addy laughed and raised her hands in surrender. "Fine. You win. I'll go away and leave you to your messy kitchen. But I warn you, if you don't get it straight by the time Sara returns, I'll have no pity for you."

"I don't want you to go away," he protested. "I need your help, Addy."

"Make up your mind, Gideon. You want my help or you don't. Which is it?"

"I do, but not as a kitchen scrubber. I need you to help me with my sausage. I need to grind a new mix of meat and rethink the ingredients. Maybe more mustard seed?"

"You're going to make *more* sausage? On top of what you've already cooked?"

"It's the only way to perfect a recipe. A rainy day like this is perfect. What we make we can save for supper and breakfast tomorrow. That way, Sara won't have to cook so much for us. I'm sure that this Joseph will like sausage. Who doesn't?"

She eyed him suspiciously. "So what, exactly, do you want me to do?"

"Help me to grind the meat and measure the spices. Taste. And watch the pan to make sure I don't burn the next batch."

"You know I didn't come here to make sausage. I have work to do for Sara."

"No sense mopping the floor until I'm done." He turned to the plate of biscuits on the counter and grabbed one. "Think fast," he said as he tossed it to her. He didn't think she'd be able to catch it, but to his surprise, Addy's hand shot out, and she snatched the biscuit midair. And before he could congratulate her, she drew back her arm, like a boy, and hurled it back at him.

He hadn't been expecting that. He made a grab, too late for the flying biscuit, and it smacked him full in the chest and broke into a dozen pieces that rained down on the floor.

Addy seemed stunned by the audacity of what she'd done. Her eyes widened, and she clapped a hand over her mouth. "Oh, Gideon. I didn't mean…" She knelt and began picking up the scattered pieces of biscuit. He did the same, but somehow, they both came up at the same instant, and their heads knocked together.

Addy began to giggle at the foolishness of it, and in seconds he, too, was laughing. He laughed so hard that tears ran down his cheeks.

"What are the two of you doing?" Ellie demanded, entering the kitchen, hands on her small hips. "Are you *kinner* to play with food like this? Sara will skin you both alive." But the last of her threat was lost in her own snicker, which became a side-slapping guffaw. Then she shook her head and returned to her sewing. "Best I have nothing at all to do with this," she threw back.

"Ya," Gideon called after her. "Better you don't." He glanced back at Addy, who was now sitting on the floor, covering her face with her hands and snickering.

"You…you're in trouble," she accused. But from the tone of her voice, he knew that she'd forgiven him and was enjoying herself immensely. "If my mother could see me—"

"Good for us she's not here."

Addy chuckled. "You have no idea."

"Maybe a little," he answered, gesturing with his thumb and forefinger. "I have an Aunt Martha, and she is a—" He stopped in midsentence, not wanting to insult Addy's mother. He'd heard a few stories about Martha Coblentz from Sara, but he wouldn't want to hurt Addy's feelings.

"She's a what?" Addy's eyes were sparkling with amusement.

"A..." He struggled to be honest without speaking ill of his own Aunt Martha. She was, for all her bad temper, a woman of faith and determination. "A woman of substance," he pronounced. "And one who does not suffer ill-behaved boys."

"Or girls?"

He nodded and grinned at her. She smiled back as he got his feet under him and reached out to take her hand and help her up. "So," he asked, "will you help me with the sausage?"

"I suppose I'll have to," she agreed reluctantly. "Because if I don't, you'll be at this all day and never get the kitchen cleaned up before Sara gets back."

Three hours and two more batches of ground pork later, Ellie, Addy and Gideon sat around the kitchen table eating bread, sausage, cheese and pickles, washed down with glasses of buttermilk. "Is it really good?" Gideon held up his sausage sandwich to make his point. "Is this the best one yet?"

Ellie chuckled. "It is, but you've stuffed us like a Christmas goose to get it." She groaned. "And not even Joseph, Sara and us combined will be able to eat all this sausage you've cooked. You'll have to go around the neighborhood begging people to take it off your hands."

Addy wanted to offer to take a plate home for her parents. Her *mam* and *dat* would love it, and it would add to the stewed tomatoes and macaroni salad that they were planning to have for supper. Since she'd started working away from the house three days of the week and sharing dinner with Sara's household, her mother had often waited to prepare the biggest meal of the day until early evening. Then the three of them would sit around the table together.

Eating together in the kitchen, just the family, was an important part of daily life. Her *dat* sometimes pointed out that in the *Englisher* world, things were different. Husbands and wives were often too busy to have breakfast, dinner and supper together. To Addy's way of thinking, it went against all the principles of family life. How else could you share your day's successes and failures? And what kind of an example did you set for children if they sat alone in front of a television?

But as much as she would have liked to take Gideon's delicious sausage home, she wouldn't ask. She didn't want to admit that many days she and her mother whipped up a meal of bread and vegetables because the pig they'd slaughtered the previous fall was long eaten, and they had already culled her hens and ducks. As a preacher, Addy's father was often invited to other people's homes for a meal, and church Sundays always included a substantial communal meal. They never went hungry at her mother's table. There were always biscuits, granola and canned fruit, but this sausage was a real treat, and Addy hoped she hadn't been greedy in eating so much of it.

"What do you think, Addy?" Gideon urged. "Too much sage?"

"Just right," she pronounced truthfully. "The best sausage I've ever eaten, even better than my cousin Anna's, and she's the best cook in Kent County. At least, the best Amish cook," she amended. "But now I'm going to do something about this kitchen because if Sara gets home and finds—"

The sound of a motor vehicle came from outside the house. Addy jumped up and went to the window. *"Ach!"* she cried. "Look! It's Sara and the new boarder. You said she wouldn't be back so early." She looked around the room, trying to see what, if anything, could be set to rights in the next moment or two. In desperation, she seized a broom and began sweeping the floor. "We're going to be in so much trouble!"

Ellie had gotten up to help, but Gideon hadn't moved. He continued to eat his sausage sandwich as though they had all the time in the world.

"What's wrong with you?" Addy demanded. "You promised you'd clean this up."

"And I will," he answered, carefully wiping his mouth with a napkin. "She's early. I'm sure Sara's seen worse."

"When have I seen worse?" Sara asked, walking in the back door.

Addy froze, broom clutched in her hand. "Sara, I'm sorry. We didn't expect…" she managed, all in a rush. "But we're cleaning up now."

Sara stood at the entrance to the utility room and calmly removed her cloak and bonnet. "I can see the three of you have been busy while I was gone," she said without a hint of amusement. "Joseph. You'll have to excuse us. We usually keep a tidier kitchen than this."

Addy stared at the tall man who came into the house behind Sara. He wasn't young, but neither was he old. Maybe her age, perhaps a few years her senior. His face was long, his chin prominent, but he had soft brown eyes. Not so beautiful as Gideon, with his perfect nose and high forehead and butter-yellow hair, but this Joseph had nice eyes and an inviting smile. Very masculine, she decided, an outdoors man…maybe a farmer, by his tan. He wore dark blue jeans, a navy blue cotton pullover shirt and black leather shoes. All properly *Plain*. His black hat had a slightly broader brim than was worn in Seven Poplars, but it was clearly Old Order Amish wear.

"A good day to you," Joseph said heartily. His words encompassed the three of them, but it seemed to Addy that his gaze lingered on her.

Addy felt her face grow warm. Was the stranger staring at her? The sudden thought that Sara might have brought this man here with the intentions of making a match between them struck her speechless. Gideon had said that morning that he thought Sara already had an idea who she'd like to match Joseph with. She opened her mouth to answer, but nothing came out, so she nodded dumbly, bobbing her head like a duck.

Ellie spoke to Joseph; Gideon offered a clear welcome in their common *Deitsch*, but she couldn't utter a sound.

"*Danki*. I'm happy to meet you," Joseph said. His voice was nice, his accent a little strange to her. He said *danki*, instead of *danke*, but the difference was so slight she might not have noticed if she hadn't been paying such close attention. Had Sara said where he was from? Not that it mattered, because one good look at the kitchen and her housekeeping and any interest in her he might have had was lost.

Gideon rose and crossed the kitchen. He offered his hand to Joseph, and the two shook. "Hungry?" Gideon asked. "We've got plenty left. I hope you like sausage."

"*Ya,*" the stranger answered. "That would be good. Sausage is my favorite." He smiled at Addy again. "Addy Coblentz. Your father is a preacher, I think?"

She nodded. What else had Sara told Joseph about her? And why was he paying so much attention to her when Ellie was far prettier than she was? Addy felt a rush of elation. She didn't know this Joseph, didn't know his prospects or if he was someone that she would like to know better. But the notion that an eligible man, one who'd come to stay with Sara for the express purpose of finding a wife, was both interesting and exciting.

Ellie was setting two more places at the table. "Would you like Addy and me to make Joseph's room ready in the bachelor quarters?" she asked Sara. "We were going to ready it up after dinner. We just didn't expect you so soon."

The room, of course, was already clean, but Joseph's bed had no linen yet. Sara had asked them to make the bed with fresh sheets and quilts. And both of them had forgotten. The bachelor's quarters, where Gideon slept, were in a separate building a short distance from the main house. Ellie had told Addy that Sara had hired carpenters to remodel what had been an enclosed shed into two comfortable rooms, because parents of her female boarders wouldn't have been comfortable having strange men sleeping under the same roof as the girls.

"I can see that you didn't," Sara replied. "The train was on time but, with the heavy rain, we decided to come straight home instead of stopping at a restaurant to eat." She looked expectantly at Addy. "Could you see to Joseph's room now? He's been traveling for many hours. I'm sure he'd like an opportunity to unpack and make himself at home."

"Ya," Addy answered. "Of course. We'll do it now." She offered Joseph a shy smile, and he grinned back at her. And as she and Ellie left the room, Addy heard him say, "You're right. She's very pretty."

The two girls hurried upstairs to the big walk-in closet that Sara used for linens. "He thinks you're pretty," Addy told Ellie in a whisper. "He said so. Didn't you hear him?"

"He wasn't talking about me, you woodenhead," Ellie replied with a giggle. *"You.* You saw how he was watching you. Sara must have brought him here to meet you."

Addy's surprise must have shown on her face, because Ellie laughed out loud.

"Ne," Addy said. "Men don't find me attractive. I'm too tall. Too much of a beanpole."

"Silly goose. How do you know what men think? I saw Joseph's eyes light up when he saw you. He likes you. Now, all you have to do is be on your best behavior, so you don't scare him off, until you can learn if you might want him to court you." Ellie climbed on a stool and took down two pillows and a log-cabin-patterned quilt. She pushed them into Addy's arms. "It isn't your looks that scare away boys. It's your tongue." She folded her arms over her small bosom and regarded her seriously. "Sometimes you're very hard on Gideon."

"Hard on him?" Addy repeated. She hugged the quilt and pillows to her chest. "I'm just being honest. Should I agree with everything he says?"

"Of course not," Ellie said, reaching up to pull down a set of sheets. "But don't be so quick to criticize men. Their feelings are easily bruised. Be yourself, Addy, but stop thinking and acting like you aren't someone that a man would want to walk out with, because that isn't true."

"You're just saying that to be nice," Addy replied.

"I'm saying it because it's so. You have to value yourself. If you don't, how will anyone else value you?" She climbed down and started for the stairs with the sheets. "No wonder you're almost thirty and not yet betrothed," she said. "You've been so certain that no one wanted to marry you that you don't give anyone a real chance."

Addy thought about Caleb as she followed Ellie. She was still certain he hadn't been the man for her, but *had* she given him a chance? "Really?"

"Really. You're smart and funny and a good friend." Ellie glanced over her shoulder as they reached the staircase. "And you may as well get used to the idea that you'll have your choice of suitors, because Sara would never have taken you on if she didn't believe in you."

Chapter Eight

Gideon guided the big sorrel mule around the long shed to the woodpile. Jasper was strong, smart and willing, and he pulled the oak log as if it weighed no more than a hundred-pound bag of feed, although it was many times heavier. His father had used horses for the farm work, but he was finding a new respect for Sara's mules each time he asked a new task of them.

Coming to Kent County and Sara Yoder's home had been his mother's idea, heartily endorsed by his father. They thought it was high time he settled down with a wife and a houseful of little woodchoppers and dishwashers. Why his *dat* would subscribe to such a notion when he hadn't married until he was well into his thirties, Gideon didn't know. Likely, his mother was to blame. He loved his mother—he adored her. But that didn't mean that he would dance to her tune like a wooden puppet on strings. A man had a right to make decisions for himself, and he would not be pushed or dragged into matrimony until he was good and ready.

That said, why was it that the time with Sara—with all these new and comely young women surrounding him—wasn't quite as much fun as he'd expected? He liked the new girls he'd met. The past two weeks, since Joseph had joined the household, had been packed with good times. He and Joseph had attended church service the past two Sundays, once here in Seven Poplars and once over in Rose Valley. Attending services somewhere every Sunday had been his idea. He'd explained to Joseph that the best way to meet girls was after worship, when there was food and conversation, and everyone was in the best of moods. Joseph had gone along with the idea because he was eager to find a wife.

And Sundays weren't the only days when a man could find a little fun. He and Joseph had taken part in a softball game on the Seven Poplars' schoolhouse playground, boys against girls, a singing at another church district and spent an evening bowling with Thomas, Menno and Titus in Dover. He'd spent the previous Saturday with Charley Byler, Thomas, Menno and Titus roofing an elder couple's house. And he'd found time to visit Spence's Sale and Auction twice, sampling the excellent sausage, cold cuts, cheese and scrapple for sale there. At Spence's he'd managed to meet several attractive young women who came down from Lancaster to work in the food stands.

Gideon had come to Delaware for the summer, expecting the people to be like sausage without sage compared to being at home with his circle of pals and cousins in Wisconsin. Instead, he'd found himself pleasantly surprised. He considered himself to be easygoing, someone who could find friends anywhere, but he'd never thought he'd come to feel so strongly about two girls that he had no intention of ever dating—Ellie and Addy. Ellie had quickly become a confidant, almost like another sister. And Addy? Addy Coblentz… He couldn't quite figure out what category to put that girl in.

He glanced at Addy, out in Sara's backyard, as he soothed the mule with soft words and loosened the metal teeth of the strap that dug into the log. If she'd seen him, she didn't let on. But how could she not? How could a woman carry rugs outside hang them over a tree branch and beat the dust out of them without noticing a fine-looking man and a big red mule not a hundred feet from her?

This was the second log he and Jasper had dragged up from the woods, and although Addy had been in the yard both times, she seemed oblivious to him. Not that he wanted her to make a fuss over him, but most girls would have seen him sweating in the hot sun and offered to bring him a glass of ice water or lemonade. Most would have found some excuse to amble over and mention a chore Sara wanted done this week or just make a remark about the weather or tonight's rematch at the schoolhouse.

The first log he'd hauled up, Gideon had seen Addy, plain as the nose on your face, eyeballing Joseph, who had been carrying an armload of kindling wood into the kitchen. She'd noticed Joseph, all right. In fact, Addy had been paying a lot of attention to Joseph since he'd come to stay at Sara's. Maybe Addy was simply being nice, Joseph being a newcomer and her wanting to make him feel welcome. But maybe it was because Addy found him attractive. It was no secret that, unlike him, Joseph had come expressly to find a wife. And anybody that wasn't blind could see that the man found Addy a likely candidate to become his life partner and helpmate. But then, Joseph seemed enthusiastic about *all* the girls. He was all smiles, mumbled compliments and eager to pursue any eligible female who looked his way.

Gideon was used to girls flocking around him, fluttering their eyelashes, laughing at *his* stories, and waiting for him to ask them if he could drive them home. He'd never been vain about his looks, but he supposed he would do. His sisters were all pretty, and he inherited the same thick yellow hair, strong body and well-formed features that they all shared. Everyone told him he was a fine figure of a man…everyone but Addy and Ellie.

And Sara. You'd have to get up early in the morning to pry a compliment that wasn't deserved out of Sara Yoder.

Sara made no mention of his height, his strength or his looks. And apparently, Addy and Ellie followed her lead. They were never critical of him, except when he and Addy were going head-to-head on subjects such as when a kitchen should be cleaned in the midst of a cooking project or how many pieces of chicken a man needed for his dinner. But both of the young women treated him more like a pesky little brother who needed to be reined in than a possible candidate for a husband.

Not that he cared.

So far, he'd never fallen head over heels for a girl, never met a woman whom he liked enough to want to spend the rest of his life with as her husband. Well, there was that one, a *maedle* that he'd almost decided to court, not because he really wanted to, but because everyone seemed to expect it. Sandra had been an excellent choice, according to all the neighbors. She was pretty, an accomplished seamstress and the daughter of a bishop. Gideon liked Sandra well enough, and he'd almost, but not quite, decided that maybe she would be the one. But then one afternoon, clearly by accident, he'd overheard her boasting to some of her girlfriends. He was no eavesdropper, but what he heard revealed something about her character that he couldn't overlook or forgive. He'd later confronted Sandra with what she'd said, and she'd freely owned up to it. They'd parted company immediately, but, because he didn't want her to face gossip, he allowed her to say that she'd rejected him. And he hadn't lost any sleep over their breakup.

So the only girl he'd even come close to walking out with hadn't confused him as much as Addy. What was it about her? She had nice eyes, *beautiful* eyes, if he was honest with himself. At first, he hadn't thought she was pretty, not like Lilly Hershberger or Violet Troyer, but the more he saw of Addy, the more he thought she had an honest, natural beauty. A beauty that would last well into middle age. She might not be as showy as some, but there was something about her that made a man take delight in watching her.

Addy was tall for a woman, and he liked that because he didn't have to crick his neck looking down at her. He'd always thought a couple looked out of place when one was tall and the other short. And Addy was slim as a willow sapling, which he found pleasing. But she perplexed him. Sometimes, just being near her gave him a stomach-ache. Nothing was ever easy with that one.

The trouble with Addy, and it was a big one, was that she never agreed with him. He never knew what she was going to say or why. And although she always listened politely when he gave his opinion, it was clear she preferred her own. Why she got under his skin, he didn't know. Addy was good company; she just always kept him guessing. She didn't act like other girls, and it was clear that she didn't understand that he was prime husband material.

Gideon stalled, watching her, pretending to adjust Jasper's harness, tightening a strap and then loosening it by the same number of holes. Addy kept her back to him. A breeze carried the dust from the rugs away from the house and away from where she was standing, but it also sent her *kapp* strings flying and it blew at the hem of her tattered burgundy dress so that she had to keep pushing the skirt down to keep from exposing her knees.

She seemed full of energy as she worked, tossing one rug after another over the branch and whacking it with the old metal beater. Cleaning rugs was a chore his sisters all hated, and often they'd cajoled and wheedled him into helping them. Rugs were heavy, but Addy carried them without hesitation, her back straight as a broomstick, her step lively. He had to admit he liked watching her work. He just wished she would take her eyes off Joseph as he went in and out of the house, going about his chores.

The mule snorted and laid his ears back, reminding Gideon that the animal might be as thirsty as he was. He led the animal to the edge of the farmyard and pumped fresh water into the horse trough. When Jasper had drunk his fill, Gideon pumped hard and fast, removed his straw hat and stuck his own head under the cool water and let it wash away the dust and sweat from his face and neck. He held his head under until his hair was wet through, and when he stood, water ran down his back and soaked through his shirt. He took the cup from the nail on the post, filled it and drank.

Addy still didn't glance in his direction. He and Jasper might have been the paint on the chicken house for all the attention she paid them.

It irked him. Was she ignoring him deliberately? Was she mad at him over something?

He began to hum and then sing the chorus of a praise hymn. Addy still didn't look at him, even when he sang louder. He knew she wasn't deaf. He ran his fingers through his hair, wrung out the water and picked up his hat. On a whim, he perched the hat on Jasper's head and laughed at his own joke.

No reaction came from Addy. Maybe, he thought, she was so wrapped up in watching Joseph that she really didn't see him. He felt foolish, showing off like a schoolboy for a girl who wasn't the least interested in him. He'd had no personal experience with such an incident, but he'd seen plenty of boys who had.

A thought struck him suddenly as he

compared himself to other boys he knew. He was smitten…

Was it possible?

Was this the way other boys felt when they liked a girl? *Really* liked a girl? Confused? Inadequate? Even sick in the belly somehow?

The thought made him take his hat back from the mule and put it on his own head.

His grandfather talked about being struck by a lightning bolt the first time he'd met *Grossmama*. Gideon certainly didn't feel as if he'd been hit by lightning, but…he *did* sometimes have a hollow sensation in his stomach and kind of a dull aching in his chest.

Love wasn't supposed to make you sick, was it?

He looked at the mule. "Maybe you've pulled enough logs for one day," he said. Taking up the reins, he guided the animal back to the barn, unhitched him and turned him out to pasture. Gideon hung up the harness and left the building, meaning to walk straight over to Addy and strike up a conversation. See if she could ignore him then. See if his wonky stomach got better or worse. But as he stepped back out into the yard, he saw that Joseph was already standing there beside her, another load of wood in his arms.

That had to be a ploy. Joseph had carried in enough wood to fill the box behind the stove twice over. Who was he fooling? He was deliberately going in and out just so he could walk by Addy and talk to her. Was it possible that Sara had already made an arrangement between the two of them? Had she successfully made a match for Addy without Gideon knowing? That would make him the fool, wouldn't it? And if Addy favored Joseph over him, what did that say?

He wondered if he had done something to show himself in a poor light.

He glanced their way again. Not that he didn't want both of them to be happy, but he knew Joseph pretty well. And he knew Addy. Sara might be the matchmaker, but Gideon wasn't so sure they would make a good couple.

He eyed them. Was he misreading the situation? Was Addy just being friendly because she was such a good person? Surely, it was too soon for *real* courtship. Joseph had only been there two weeks. And he hadn't even taken her home from a singing, or been a supper guest at Addy's mother's table.

His thoughts tumbling, Gideon turned away and retraced his steps in the direction of the wood lot where he'd been taking down dead trees. His stomach felt worse now than before. At the edge of the hardwoods he'd seen a patch of late-flowering dogwood. The blossoms were prettier than usual that year, and for some reason that he didn't understand, they'd made him think of Addy in her starched white prayer *kapp*. Not fancy yard flowers, but hardy, independent, stubborn even, coming back up even after they'd been cut down.

When he reached the dogwood trees, on impulse, he took out his penknife and carefully cut off a half-dozen multiblossomed branches. He was cutting them for Addy, though he wasn't sure why.

He hoped she wouldn't laugh. What he hoped, he realized, was that she'd carry the bouquet home and put it in her room. That way, his gift would be the last thing she'd see before she turned out the lamp and the first thing she'd admire in the morning.

Not that he was feeling romantic toward Addy. He hadn't changed his mind about courting anybody. It was just a matter of having her notice him. He liked her, sure, liked her a lot. Certainly as a friend. The notion that what he felt for Addy might be something more nudged at the back of his mind, but he tamped it down.

It could be that he was just looking out for a pal. Maybe he was simply making sure that Addy realized that more than one fellow might admire her. She didn't have to take the first potential husband Sara dangled in front of her. Even if Joseph was a nice boy. She could have her pick, couldn't she?

He went over Addy's attributes as he

walked back to the house with the bunch of flowering dogwood. She was a spirited, hard worker who had a special talent for tasting food and knowing what spices were in it, a trait he especially admired. He had it, his father and two of his sisters did, but Gideon had never known anyone outside his family to share the gift. Addy was a little plain-spoken for a woman. Was that a positive or a negative? Some men might not like that, but he was different. Raised with all those sisters, he'd become used to girls who had strong opinions.

Of necessity, he'd adopted his father's way of thinking. "Wood and stone make a house, but a woman makes a home," his father always said. He'd left most things in their home, other than family worship practices, to their mother. *Mam* had decided what must be purchased for the household, what needs her children had and how long they would remain in school.

Where most children left formal education at age fourteen, at the end of eighth grade, his mother had insisted that he and his sisters continue their studies for another full year. His mother had taught school before she was married, and she was well-read. She'd even made regular submissions to *The Budget*, and she'd insisted that her children spend some time every day reading or practicing their math. His father always said that his *mam* had more than her share of common sense, and he'd advised Gideon to find a bride with an equally good mind. Gideon wondered what his parents would think of someone like Addy. Would they see the prickly exterior, or would they recognize what a fine, strong woman she was?

As he neared the house, Gideon began to grow nervous. Was it proper to offer Addy flowers? Would she be offended, or worse, would she laugh at him? Maybe Seven Poplars fellows didn't give girls flowers. His mother had always told them that his *dat* had gotten her attention when, in the third grade, he'd picked her an armful of black-eyed Su-

sans with a honeybee tangled in the blossoms. The bee had stung her, and she teased
his *dat* to this day that he'd done it on purpose because she'd beaten him in a spelling
bee that morning. Gideon had looked through
the dogwood blossoms for bees, even though
he'd never seen bees around dogwood. He
didn't want history to repeat itself.

When Gideon reached the back porch, he
found that the yard was empty, and he stood
there with the bouquet in his hands, wondering what to do. Should he put them in the
kitchen sink for Sara? Or would it be better
to just toss them into the chicken pen and
forget the whole thing? He didn't want to
make a bigger fool of himself, and the idea
of giving Addy the flowers was beginning
to seem worse by the moment.

Just as he was about to cut and run, the
back door opened, and Ellie came out with
a dishpan of potato peelings. "Gideon. I
was just taking these out to the pigs. Would
you mind? I've got a pot of potato soup on

the stove, and I don't want the milk to boil over." He knew she'd seen the flowers, but she didn't ask why he was carrying them.

"Ya," he said quickly. "I can do that. Sure." *What to do with the dogwood branches?* He couldn't carry both the dishpan of peelings and the bouquet, and he didn't want to leave the arrangement on the porch. Who knew who would come along and ask questions? And what if Joseph found them, took them in and gave them to Addy himself?

"Nice dogwood blossoms," Ellie remarked. "I imagine that's the last of the blooms. Getting too warm." Her bottom lip was twitching. He could see the amusement in her eyes.

Sweat began to trickle down the back of Gideon's neck. His father was right. He was impulsive. Why had he cut flowers for a girl he had no intention of courting? "Are those for Sara?" Ellie asked.

He couldn't lie, but his tongue stuck to the roof of his mouth. He couldn't bring himself to say they were for Addy, so he just shook his head.

Now Ellie's lips curved into a smile. "Not for me, I hope. Dogwood makes me sneeze."

Agony. He looked at the ground. Seconds passed. What was wrong with him? When had he ever been tongue-tied in front of a girl? Again, he shook his head.

Ellie took pity on him. "For Addy? She'll love them. Tomorrow's her birthday. Did you know that? Tonight, after she goes home, I'm going to bake her a birthday cake."

He let his breath out with a whoosh of relief. *"Ya,"* he stammered. "F-for her birthday." He shoved the flowers toward Ellie.

With all the grace that he lacked, Ellie placed the pan of potato peels on the step and gathered the dogwood branches in her arms. "How thoughtful of you," she said.

Gideon scooped up the dishpan and made his escape, but he hadn't gone more than a dozen yards when he heard the squeak of the screen door and Addy's squeal.

"*Danke*, Gideon!" she called after him. "They're beautiful!"

"Nobody ever gave me flowers before," Addy exclaimed to Ellie. "I love dogwoods, and these blossoms are so pretty." She felt a rush of excitement. Was it possible that things were changing for her?

"They are," Ellie agreed as she held the door for her friend. "I told you that Gideon likes you."

Addy looked down at the bouquet. She was almost too thrilled to stand still. "I suppose he does, as a friend, but he doesn't *like* like me."

"*Lecherich*! Ridiculous. Of course he likes you, silly goose." She took a long-handled wooden spoon off the counter and stepped up on her stool to stir the potato soup. "No young man ever brought me flowers, although one did leave a half gallon of strawberry ice cream on my windowsill once." Ellie giggled. "It melted into a big puddle before I discovered it. A waste of good ice cream."

"Are they for my birthday? Is that why Gideon cut the dogwoods for me?"

"I told him it was your birthday tomorrow," Ellie explained, "but that was after he brought the bouquet."

Addy glanced down at the flowers, touched, but not entirely sure what to make of it. "I…I don't know what *Mam* will say."

Ellie took a clean spoon, dipped it into the simmering soup and blew on what she'd dipped out. "You don't think she'll approve of Gideon?" She tasted the soup. "*Ach.* Still hot, but I think it needs salt." Remnants of celery and half an onion sat on the counter. "Would you like to taste it?"

"*Ne*, you make good soup. My mother always puts in too much salt. Maybe we could just put the salt shaker on the table and let everyone salt it to suit themselves."

Ellie nodded, then arched one dainty eyebrow quizzically. "You didn't answer me. You think your parents wouldn't like Gideon? Because he's a hired hand?"

Addy sighed. "It sounds awful, doesn't it,

that she wouldn't want me to marry a poor boy. But…" She looked around to make certain they were alone. "It isn't that *Mam* is a greedy person. She's not. But things have been hard for her. She wants more for me. 'Why not choose a husband with a good farm or a steady trade?' she always says. They have no savings, Ellie, nothing put away for their old age. It will be up to me to care for them, and a poor boy…" She swallowed, her mouth suddenly dry. "It's not for me so much as them." She glanced down at her patched skirt and the threadbare sneakers with the hole in one toe. "I'm used to doing without. I don't mind, but I don't want to see *Mam* and *Dat* suffer when they can no longer care for themselves."

Ellie considered and then nodded. "I understand."

"*Ya*, but no matter how I say it, it comes out wrong," she admitted. No one had questioned her cousin Anna when she'd accepted Samuel Mast's proposal. Samuel's acres were fertile, and his house substantial. And hadn't their grandmother smiled and offered words of praise when each of Anna's sisters had married well? Why, then, did she have to feel ashamed that she was looking for someone who could offer her family and her children security?

"Your mother is looking out for your best interests. It's what parents do," Ellie said. "And I can't blame you for not wanting to go against your parents' wishes." She smiled. "But they should have nothing against Joseph. And I heard him ask you if he could walk you home from the softball game tonight."

Addy opened a cabinet door and removed a crockery pitcher. Carefully, she arranged the dogwood blossoms in it, pleased at how pretty they looked in the blue-spatter container. "Maybe I'd best leave these here for Sara to enjoy," she said, thinking that whether she took them home or not, nothing could change the fact that Gideon had brought them for her.

"Well?" Ellie asked. "Are you going to

walk home with Joseph? That should please your mother."

"Haven't decided if I'm going." She put the pitcher in the center of the table, stood back and admired it.

"Oh, you're going if I have to drag you there." Ellie turned off the gas burner under the potato soup. "The boys beat the girls twenty to two the other night. Lilly's pitching is terrible, and she's better than Mary. I think your cousin Miriam is supposed to be good, but her sister Grace told me that she and Charley are expecting again, so Miriam can't play. And Charley said that you could pitch like a boy, better than him, he said. So we need you, and you can't let us down."

"Can't *you* pitch?" Addy asked, feeling uneasy. She *could* throw a softball, but she didn't like the idea of standing in the middle of everyone, being the center of attention.

"I can pitch better than Lilly, but I'm the catcher. Please. It will be fun. I promise." She grinned. "And maybe Gideon and Joseph will *both* want to walk you home."

Chapter Nine

"Strike Gideon out!" Miriam Yoder shouted. "One more! One more!" Miriam and her sister, Susanna, had leaped up out of their folding chairs and waved their arms. Lots of people had come to watch the softball game, including Addy's father, whom she spotted standing behind Anna Yoder.

It was the bottom of the seventh inning, and the score was tied five to five. The fellows had two outs, Thomas was the runner on third and Joseph was on first. Everyone seemed to be having a great time, but Addy wished she were anywhere but there. Her hands were sweating, and her knees felt weak. So far, she hadn't made a fool of herself pitching, but she was afraid that she would. The last two times Gideon had been up to bat, he'd hit the ball over the school-yard fence and into the cow pasture. The determined look on his face told her that he intended to hit another home run.

Gideon was watching Addy, the bat clenched between his hands and a grin on his face. She was pretty sure she could strike him out, she just had to pitch the ball low and inside. She knew he would hate to be shown up by a girl, though, and for a second, she wondered if maybe she should throw a fat pitch down the middle of the plate, one he could definitely hit. Thomas would get home for sure, and if Gideon hit the ball far enough, he and Joseph might do the same. Was that the sensible thing to do for a girl who didn't want to end up a spinster?

The thought didn't linger long enough for Addy to catch her breath. If Bishop Atlee had been at bat, she would have tried to strike him out. In softball—Amish or English—

you played fair and tried your best. Doing anything less, even to please a man, would have been wrong. Over the years, there were things she'd said and done that she might not have been proud of, but she'd never been dishonest.

Behind Gideon, Ellie, who was catching, reached down and tapped her ankle. She had the same idea that Addy had. Addy pitched the ball low and inside. The edge of Gideon's bat connected with the ball. The ball hit the ground hard a few yards ahead of him and rolled toward the pitcher's mound. Gideon dropped the bat and ran toward first. Addy ran, scooped up the ball and threw it to Ellie.

Thomas ran as hard as he could toward the home plate, but Ellie darted out and tagged him. He scooped up Ellie and kept running, then he tripped and they both went down. Everyone ran toward them to see if either one of them was hurt, but both came up covered in dust and laughing. Ellie still had the ball clutched in her glove, and Thomas owned up that he was out, fair and square. Some of the boys were calling for another inning, but everyone was laughing and shouting. Amidst the general excitement from both teams, the umpire, Anna's husband, Samuel, declared the game officially a tie, then invited both teams back to his house for homemade root beer, ice cream and his wife's famous donuts.

The boys gathered up the balls, mitts and bats and stowed them in the compartment under the schoolhouse, and then everyone trekked down the lane to the Mast farmhouse. On the big wraparound porch, a group of neighborhood men, mostly fathers of the ballplayers, were pouring paper cups of root beer and bringing donuts and other treats from the house.

"Surprise," Addy's *grossmama* called from her rocking chair. "It's an upside-down frolic." And the dozens of children, some barely able to toddle, jumped up and down, clapped and cheered.

The other young people seemed as astonished as Addy. She couldn't remember being

at an *upside-down* frolic for years. It meant
that the women sat and were waited on while
the men and boys served the refreshments
and cleaned up the mess. As Addy, Ellie and
the rest of the girls rounded the house and
saw the side yard, it was evident that a lot of
planning had gone into the surprise. Someone had set up tables, not in long rows as was
normal for communal meals, but placed here
and there under the trees among the blankets
spread on the ground. Addy caught sight of
Sara near the back door. When Sara noticed
Addy, she waved and hurried toward her.

"I'm sorry I missed the softball," Sara said.
"But I'm glad I caught you. There's someone I want you to meet. Nathan King. He's
visiting Bishop Atlee's family. Nathan is a
cousin of the bishop's wife. He's from west-
ern Maryland."

Addy looked at her questioningly. "Is he…"

"Looking for a wife? He is. Nathan's a
widower, but he's a little older than I'd like
for you. His children are grown and out of
the house, all but a daughter, fifteen. Still,

he owns a nice butcher shop and is well-established. The bishop vouches for his character and situation." She motioned for Addy to walk with her. "No need for you to be nervous. I'll make arrangements for you to meet him. Nathan isn't here this evening. He's at the bishop's home with a toothache. And just as well, because Joseph asked your father for permission to walk you home."

Addy was still trying to imagine the older Nathan King. She could picture him in her mind as a stout man in a white apron stained with blood. Now the image of a swollen jaw and him clamping an ice bag came to her. She looked at Sara. "He did?"

"He did, indeed. He's anxious to please, our Joseph. Doesn't want to offend your parents. Wants to do everything right."

Addy paused to brush dust off her apron. "Does *Mam* know?"

"*Ya*, she's the one who told me. Naturally, she had questions about Joseph's prospects. He's not so well-fixed as the butcher, but he could pay your fee, and he has a half interest in a house left to him and his brother by a grandfather."

Two men interested in her at the same time? No wonder her mother had appeared happy.

"I know that Joseph told you he sells livestock, mostly cattle, and he's got a small farm. If you chose Joseph, it's only fair to tell you, though, that he takes care of his brother. I understand that the brother's not able to live on his own, an unfortunate accident when he was a child." She smiled reassuringly and touched Addy's cheek. "You'd not have to take care of him, other than in a normal way as part of the household. He's able physically and no burden. But Joseph tells me that his brother will never marry. I didn't think you would consider that a problem. Am I correct?"

"Of course it wouldn't be a problem." They had stopped to stand under a pin oak in the backyard. All around Addy, she could hear the sounds of laughter and people enjoying each other's company. "If I…" She felt herself flush with embarrassment. "I mean if we..." She took a deep breath. "I didn't know that Joseph was interested in me...in *that* way."

"How could you not know? The way he hangs on every word you say and spends his whole workday trying to put himself in your path?" Sara rested her fists on her hips and chuckled. "I don't know where your mother got the idea that you'd be difficult to match. Nothing wrong with you that a little polishing won't cure. I think you've been your own greatest obstacle, Addy."

"You really think so?" she asked. Was it possible that she wasn't as hopeless as she'd believed?

"You should know by now that I don't give unearned praise, Addy. You're a good girl. You've average looks, but you carry yourself well, and you have strength of character. I've told you before, it's what's inside that counts. And before any man can love you, you must love yourself."

Addy nodded slowly.

"I'll not speak against your mother," Sara said, lowering her voice. "She wants the best for you, and she's had a hard life. It's only natural for her only daughter that she'd want more for you than she had herself. But…" Sara sighed. "Martha can be critical, more so with you, I think, because she sees herself in you." Her eyes narrowed. "You aren't your mother, and you have no need to take the first man who asks you to wed him. You'll not be an old spinster."

Addy looked down at the woman who was not just her employer anymore, but her friend. "You promise?"

"I give you my word, Addy. So long as you listen to reason, I'll find you a good match." She winked mischievously. "And maybe one better than you ever hoped for."

"Why did you ask my father if you could walk me home?" Addy asked Joseph as he helped her over the stile that led into her Aunt Hannah's cow pasture. This wasn't the same stile that had broken and caused her so much grief the first day she'd met Gideon. No one had ever allowed *this* stile to become unsafe, because her Uncle Jonas had built it, and her cousins' husbands kept it in good repair.

Crossing Aunt Hannah's farm was the best way home to Addy's house from Anna and Samuel's by foot. Her cousin and Samuel had the farm closest to the schoolhouse, and this was the path that Addy had always taken as a child going to school. These sturdy steps had taken her from nervous six-year-old to a young woman; she'd climbed them twice a day until she'd graduated from the eighth grade.

"You should have asked me, instead of asking my father," she told Joseph as she released his hand, once she reached the ground on the far side of the fence. They began walking across the field. "Or you might have asked Ellie to speak for you."

"I'm sorry. I wasn't sure." Joseph kept pace beside her, but maintained a seemly distance between them. It was twilight, but not yet dark. "I was introduced to your father, and I just thought..." He looked at her. "Would you have said yes if I'd just walked right up to you and asked you?"

"I would have," she answered honestly. She liked Joseph, but whether she liked him *enough* was the question. He talked a lot, but she didn't feel as though she knew him. He seemed a good person, kind, and he worked hard. He definitely had her respect, but... The thought came to her that he wasn't Gideon, and she was a little shocked. Why would she be comparing a perfectly good suitor to Gideon?

"*Goot.* I didn't know whether you would or not," Joseph went on. "I didn't know if you and Gideon..."

Gideon! Now Joseph was talking about Gideon. Was he the center of everything? Sure, this evening he'd had his usual circle of admiring girls at the horseshoe pits, and he'd eaten his cake and ice cream with a bevy of giggling, eligible young women at his table. But that was no affair of hers. If they wanted to fuss over him, what did it matter? They were friends, nothing more.

"If Gideon and I what?" she asked, her voice a little cross. Instantly, Sara's warning came to her, and she forced herself to speak more kindly. "Why would you think that Gideon had any attachment to me?"

He shrugged. "The two of you seem… seem so easy together, as if you've known each other a long time. Or had an agreement."

"Ne," she protested. "He is a nice person, and we work together. That's all."

"Goot," Joseph repeated. "Watch out." He grabbed her arm and pulled her to one side. "The cows," he said, pointing to a dark pile on the ground.

"Danke. I didn't notice." It was almost dark. Easy to miss where the cows had been. Had she stepped into it, her shoe would have been a mess.

"That's the one trouble with crossing a pasture at night," Joseph said, and then chuckled at his joke. "Cow pies."

She wasn't sure how to answer so she didn't say anything. For years, she'd dreamed of a young man asking to walk her home or to drive her in his rig, but now that it had happened, it wasn't as much fun as she'd thought it would be. Joseph was obviously uncomfortable, as well. Maybe because all he could think to talk about was cow pies?

"Tell me about your brother," she said, changing the conversation.

"His name is Howard."

"Is he your only brother?" she asked. She had the feeling that Joseph might reach out to take her hand, but she wasn't sure she would let him. She liked Joseph fine, but was that enough? Lilly certainly didn't mind going home with different suitors. And her cousin Miriam had shocked everyone by walking out with not one but two different beaus at the same time. So why was this so difficult?

"*Ya.* We have three sisters. They're all married. One of them would take Howard if…if my wife didn't feel comfortable with him in the house. But he is happiest when things stay the same. Howard has slept in the same bedroom and eaten at the same table all his life. My grandparents raised us after my parents died."

"I'm sorry," she said. She couldn't imagine losing both her mother and father.

"I didn't really know them. I was very young when... They were driving home from an auction. There was a tornado. The team survived. I always thought that was a blessing. That the horses lived." He shrugged again. "I think they were *goot* people. My sisters say so, and Howard cried for a long time. But I don't remember much, just my grandmother and grandfather."

"So Howard is older than you?"

"Five years. The girls are older still. You would like Howard. He's *goot* at growing things. You should see his garden. He was with them, you see. I was at home with my grandmother because I had the measles. They didn't find Howard until the next day, and he was hurt badly. Before the accident, they said that he knew his letters and could count to one hundred. But after…his mind didn't work so well. He was caught under a tree branch. He has a scar on his head, but it's in his hair and doesn't show."

"I can tell that you care for him very much," she said, wanting Joseph to go on talking. It was easier than the awkward silence.

"*Ya*, I do. He is a *goot* brother. Always patient. Happy. Very clean. He doesn't talk a lot. And he never complains about my cooking."

Addy wondered if Howard was the reason Joseph hadn't married. Did other women have a problem with the idea of marrying a man with such responsibilities? It didn't sound like a bad thing to her, having such a brother-in-law. She'd heard that among the English, relatives were sometimes sent away to live with strangers, but not among the *Plain* people. They cared for their own, she thought, and it seemed right.

If she and Joseph came to an understanding, she wouldn't let Howard stand in the way of her accepting. But…but it wasn't Howard that was holding her back. She almost sighed out loud.

Why wasn't it enough that a decent man like Joseph wanted to court her? She could respect him, and her mother always said that respect was most important. First, there must be a consensus of faith, then respect and finally love. So why wasn't she more excited by the prospect? By the presence of Joseph walking with her?

By the time they reached her Aunt Hannah's farmyard, the house and barn and outbuildings were in deep shadow. But it didn't matter. Addy didn't need a flashlight. She knew the way home like the back of her hand: along the lane that led past her aunt's orchard, through the woods and onto her father's farm.

When they reached the orchard, the only light came from the crescent moon rising in the sky. Joseph's hand closed over hers, and she let him. He stopped, and she had no choice but to stop. "Addy…" He turned to face her, standing very close.

He's going to kiss me, she thought. I should stop him. Her heart was pounding; her throat constricted. *He is.* Any minute now and—

Joseph's lips brushed hers. It wasn't an unpleasant sensation, but it made her vaguely uncomfortable. She didn't go weak-kneed like she'd heard other girls talk about. Her mouth didn't even tingle. She just stood there, not sure what to do next.

Joseph moved away. *"Danki,"* he said.

Now she felt even more awkward than before. And disappointed. "We…we'd better go," she stammered. "My mother and father will be expecting me."

"Ya."

They walked on in silence, and finally Joseph said, "I want to tell you…I don't make a habit of kissing girls."

What did he want her to say? Was she supposed to tell him that he was a good kisser? Was he? She'd never kissed a boy before. How would she know? But she had the suspicion that the kiss should have been better than that. She quickened her step.

"Do you think that we... That the two of us..." He broke off. "You are a nice girl, Addy, a pretty girl and a *goot* softball pitcher."

"And you are a good man. I like you, Joseph, and I think I would like Howard, but..."

He sighed loudly and chuckled in the darkness. "But there is no lightning between us."

"Exactly." Something tight loosened in her chest, and she giggled. "There is no lightning."

"But it's better we should learn this now."

She smiled and nodded. "Exactly," she repeated. "And you deserve better."

"Not *better*," he corrected her. "Just someone different. For both of us."

"Someone different for both of us," she agreed, having even more respect for him now. "Friends?"

"Friends," Joseph agreed. And then after a moment, he said, "Was it wrong that I kissed you? I meant no disrespect."

"I think it was right," she said, and meant every word. "I think it was exactly right. And if Sara finds you a girl who makes lightning for you, I will be honored to come to your wedding."

Chapter Ten

"I don't know how to thank you young people for this," Willard said. "It's kind of you to take your Saturday to help me out. If it wasn't for my bad knee, I could do it myself ." The man tugged at his scraggly gray beard, propped his cane against the wood box and dropped onto a weathered bench to watch.

"It's no trouble at all," Gideon said, trying to speak around the three nails he was holding in his mouth. More than two weeks had passed since the softball game, and it seemed as if, day by day, he'd become more a part of the Seven Poplars community.

Today, he, Joseph, Thomas and a younger man named Andy were repairing Willard Troyer's kitchen and back porch, which had been damaged by a fire.

Willard, a widower in his seventies, lived alone. He was in good physical shape for a man his age, but he'd recently been kicked by a cow and was recovering from a knee injury. The fire had been started by lightning. A strike had ignited a maple tree beside the house, and a falling branch had set the porch roof ablaze. Fortunately, a downpour had accompanied the thunderstorm, extinguishing the fire and limiting the damage to a scorched back door, a broken window and a smoke-stained kitchen wall and ceiling. The porch roof hadn't fared as well, but the main structure of the home was fine, and Willard and his three house cats were unharmed.

Since Old Order Amish didn't believe in insurance, Willard's neighbors and church community pitched in to help. Samuel Mast had taken up a collection to buy new building materials, and the four young men had come to repair the damage. Three girls— Addy, Ellie and Jane—had volunteered to do the interior painting. Gideon didn't know Jane well, and this was the first time that he'd met Andy, but Joseph and Jane had been seeing a lot of each other in the past week. Gideon assumed that Jane had come because Joseph would be there. Andy was from another church district in the county.

Gideon was busy repairing the back steps, and Joseph was nailing shingles on the roof. Willard kept up a steady conversation, talking about how much he missed his late wife's cooking, the Japanese beetles on his crookneck squash, the sermon a visiting bishop had preached on forgiveness and the high price of everything. Gideon nodded, made appropriate remarks whenever Willard paused for breath and generally paid little attention to his chatter, which had been running nonstop since they'd arrived at eight that morning. It hadn't taken long for Gideon to realize that once Willard covered his current subjects, he'd begin repeating himself, stating almost word for word his exact opinions and smacking his cane on the floorboards to emphasize key points.

Gideon hoped he wasn't being rude by not being more attentive to the older man. It was obvious that Willard was lonely and eager to talk, and Gideon felt compassion for him. Coming from such a big family, Gideon couldn't imagine waking up each morning to a quiet house, having no one with whom to share his meals, chores and leisure time. In the course of the morning, Gideon learned from Joseph that more than a year had passed since Willard's wife had died, and that she'd been an invalid for a while before that. Willard had a snug little house, a big garden and didn't appear to be wanting for money. He wondered why Willard hadn't remarried. Very few Amish men in good health remained single, and Willard seemed fit, other than his recent mishap. Most widowers, even those who were on in years, didn't go long without finding a like-minded widow to join them in matrimony.

Joseph had certainly wasted no time in moving on to another young woman once he and Addy had decided that they weren't cut out for one another. After Addy—and Gideon hadn't been able to figure out what had happened between her and Joseph after the softball game—Sara had introduced him to a girl from Ohio whose family was visiting relatives in Kent County.

Joseph seemed pleased with her, and asked to see her again, but apparently the young woman already had an agreement with a farmer that her parents weren't aware of when they'd contacted Sara. So Joseph struck out with the Ohio girl, too. Undaunted, Sara had immediately invited the Stutzmans to supper, and Joseph and Jane seemed to have an instant attraction to each other.

So Joseph had lost two potential brides-to-be, while Sara hadn't yet found anyone for him. Gideon wasn't sure how he felt about that. He didn't want a wife any more than

Ellie wanted a husband. He had no intention of returning to Wisconsin with a bride. But Sara had promised his parents that she'd find him a match, and he couldn't help feeling just a little neglected that she hadn't even tried…especially since she'd outdone herself on Addy's behalf. Suddenly, Sara was producing one prospective husband after another, like a magician pulling rabbits out of a hat.

First there was Joseph. Then came Nathan King, too old and set in his ways to make a good match for Addy, in Gideon's opinion. Why Sara had thought the butcher a possibility, Gideon couldn't imagine. Nathan had come to Saturday dinner, immediately after Addy's stroll home with Joseph, and he wasn't what any of them had expected. Not a broad and smiling man, but tall, pinch-faced, thin as a rail and concerned more with asking Sara about Addy's work ethic than trying to get to know her. And when he wasn't asking pointed questions, he ran on and on about his prosperous business and his status as deacon in his church.

Addy had been polite, seemingly giving Nathan the benefit of the doubt, as he was a stranger and a guest, and had even attempted to turn the conversation to recipes for scrapple. But Nathan seemed ignorant of the process. His wife had always taken care of that, he'd said, and now he had a hired hand. Nathan had abruptly interrupted Addy's question about his meat-grinding process to criticize her lavender dress. He disapproved of the color, considering it too fancy for a *Plain* woman and not anything that he would ever permit a wife of his to wear. And as if that wasn't crass enough, Nathan sprinkled his ramblings with awkward attempts at humor about Ellie's lack of height.

The butcher stayed long past the time he should have made a gracious departure, ate enough dinner for two blacksmiths, ending with two enormous slices of German chocolate cake and a quarter of a cherry pie. When he was gone, Gideon, Ellie, Sara and Addy had discussed Nathan's behavior. The four of them all agreed: cousin to the bishop's wife or not, he wasn't suitable material for Addy or any of Sara's prospective brides. Sara had brought out her black book, drew a thick line through the name of Nathan King, and they all had laughed over the experience.

After the butcher's blessed departure, Sara brought up the possibility of a widower with five small children in Pennsylvania for Addy. This candidate, a bricklayer, had been unwilling to come to Delaware, but offered to pay Addy's way to visit his community to be inspected by his mother, his sister and the elders of his church. Addy had wisely turned him down, sight unseen, saying that she wasn't a cow at auction, and if the bricklayer didn't have time to come to Seven Poplars, she didn't have time to travel there. Sara had concurred, crossing him off her list, as well.

Gideon took the last nail out of his mouth, set it and drove it into the oak support. Taking a half-dozen more nails, he turned his attention to the railing. When he was finished, the stairs would be better than before the fire. He was proud of his craftsmanship. His father had taught him that if a thing wasn't worth doing right, it wasn't worth doing at all.

He wondered why Sara didn't look at her matchmaking for Addy the same way. Addy deserved the best. Surely, there was someone out there who could overlook her sometimes prickly exterior to see the beautiful, caring and bright woman beneath. She should have a husband who would cherish her, who could provide for her, someone as strong in their faith as she was. If Sara was so good at her job of finding the best match for each of her candidates, why hadn't she done better for Addy?

And now, Sara had dragged in this Andy Mast, a distant cousin of Thomas. Gideon set another nail. He knew he should be listening to Willard and paying more attention to his task, but his thoughts kept going back to Andy. Thomas's cousin claimed to be twenty-four, looked nineteen, and while able enough at laying shingles on a roof, didn't appear to Gideon to be the smartest piglet in the pen. This wet-behind-the-ears boy was obviously smitten with Addy, because he'd already taken her to a singing in his own district, and driven her home from church in an open courting buggy. Gideon couldn't say what it was about the boy he distrusted, but he instinctively felt that Andy wasn't right for Addy. He seemed too eager, too impulsive, proof of which being that when Andy found out that she would be painting here at Willard's today, he'd suddenly felt compelled to volunteer for the workday.

"I *said*, why is it that you've not taken a wife?" Willard's raised voice penetrated Gideon's musings. "You're long past the age. I can't imagine that your mother and father would be pleased to have a healthy young whelp like you with his feet still under their table. Haven't your community elders reminded you of your responsibility to…

provide for a *goot* woman…to start your own family?"

Gideon glanced up so quickly that he took his eyes off what he was doing. The hammer head struck the nail off center, bounced off and came down on his thumb. He gasped, dropped the hammer and grabbed his thumb. Gideon clenched his teeth, not wanting to appear like a wimp, but his thumb hurt. Bad. Blood seeped between his fingers. He ventured a quick look and involuntarily shuddered. "Jerusalem."

Thomas hooted. "Hit the nail, Wisconsin, not your finger!"

Gideon wanted to throw back a jaunty taunt, but all he could think of was the pain radiating out of his thumb. He glanced at it again. *Ya.* He would probably lose the nail. Stupid. Stupid, not to watch what he was doing.

"Maybe you should be painting with the girls," Thomas teased. "The worst you could do is whack yourself with a brush."

Gideon grinned back at him. Thomas

meant no offense, and he took none. If Thomas had been the one to hammer his finger, he'd probably have given him an equally hard time. The thumb was pounding now; the bleeding continued.

"First rule of a carpenter," Willard advised. "Watch what you're doing."

Good advice, Gideon thought, but a little late.

"Somebody better get a wet cloth!" Willard ordered. "Gideon's bleeding on my new steps!"

"Sorry." Gideon moved his hand away and glanced down at the step. No blood that he could see. It was all running down his arm. And some had dribbled onto his jeans. "No need for anybody to wait on me. I think there's a little ice left in my cooler. I'll just put some of that on my thumb." They'd stopped at a little market that morning and bought ice for their packed lunches. Still holding his thumb, Gideon walked into the kitchen. The first thing he saw was Addy on her knees, painting the molding that ran along the floor. Andy was there, close beside her, a brush in his hand, showing her how to use a piece of cardboard to keep from getting paint on the wall. Much too close, to Gideon's way of thinking.

"I've had an accident," he declared.

"You're hurt?" Addy started to get up. Andy was ahead of her, reaching out to take her hand, helping her to her feet. She paid him no mind, but hurried across the kitchen. "How bad is it? What did you do?"

Andy followed her, and stopped not a foot behind her. He was no longer holding her hand, but he seemed to be standing nearer than was proper. It wasn't like Addy to allow such familiarity, Gideon thought, but she did seem at ease with Andy, laughing at his jokes, paying attention to every word he said.

Gideon sank into a chair. "I need ice," he said between clenched teeth. "In the cooler."

"I'll get it," Ellie offered.

Addy leaned over his hand. "Let me see."

He gave her a stoic look. "I hit my thumb with the hammer. I think it's broken." The thumb was already turning black-and-blue, but the bleeding had become a slow ooze.

Andy rested his hand on Addy's shoulder and peered down. "It's probably not broken," he said, helpfully. "My brother split his thumb in half with a hatchet when he was chopping kindling. It looked a lot worse than that."

Thomas and Willard came into the kitchen and took a look. Willard whistled. Thomas just shook his head.

"I think you'd better go home and clean it up," Ellie said when she returned with some ice wrapped in a cloth towel. "Do you know when you last had a tetanus shot?"

"Since Christmas," Gideon replied. "Sometime in February. I stepped on a nail."

"In February?" Andy chuckled. "Wisconsin winters must be a lot warmer than Delaware. Not much running barefoot here in February."

Gideon didn't comment. His mother and sisters had given him plenty of grief about the stupidity of being out on the side porch in his bare feet when there was snow on the ground. He was feeling foolish now, and just a little sick to his stomach. "Maybe I should call it quits for the day."

Thomas nodded. "We can finish up here. Go and see what Sara thinks. Doubt if a doctor could do much for you. I think it would look worse if it was broken."

Gideon glanced at Addy. "I hate to ask, but would you mind driving me home? I feel a little lightheaded."

"That's a good idea," Ellie said. "I'll finish this trim, clean up the kitchen and catch a ride home with Thomas." She looked at Thomas, and he nodded.

"Maybe Ellie should drive you," Andy suggested. "I'd be glad to take Addy home."

"You live in the opposite direction," Gideon protested. He looked to Addy. "Jasper might be a little hard for Ellie to handle."

"*Ya.*" Addy sighed. "I'd better take you."

Gideon thought he caught a note of disappointment in her voice. Had she planned on having Andy drive her? Surely, his injury should come before the boy's need to show off that fast black horse of his.

Fifteen minutes later, Gideon and Addy were in Sara's buggy, heading down Willard's lane. When Gideon looked back, he saw Andy Mast standing on the porch staring wistfully after them. Gideon sat on the passenger's side of the front seat, Addy next to him, holding the reins. Jasper gave no trouble, and Gideon hadn't expected any. Jasper was always somewhat reluctant to leave home, but always eager to get back to his stable. As traffic-wise as the mule was, it wouldn't have surprised him if Jasper could have pulled the buggy home to Sara's without a driver.

Gideon settled against the backrest, his hurting hand cradled in his lap. Addy had wrapped it in a towel with ice and put another, bigger towel around it. The pain in his thumb was a steady ache, but he didn't really believe it was broken. He tried not to smile as he watched Addy from the corner of his eye. She sat there, tall and confident, completely in control as she eased the animal out onto the blacktop road.

"It's a shame you hurt yourself," she sympathized. "A smashed thumb can really hurt."

"Ya," he agreed. "It can."

"But I doubt if it's broken."

He grunted, unwilling to yield the advantage. "Maybe not, but it's better to be safe than sorry." And getting her away from that Andy Mast was definitely better for her, whether she realized that he was looking out for her or not.

The Friday after Gideon's accident at Willard's, Addy and her mother and father arrived at her Aunt Hannah's home for a family celebration. Addy's cousin Susanna was married to David King, and the couple lived with Aunt Hannah and her new husband. Both Susanna and David had been born with Down syndrome and needed help with everyday life. They were a loving couple, and their marriage—despite her aunt's worries—was going well.

It was David's birthday, and Addy was certain that the gathering in his honor would thrill both him and Susanna. David's parents lived nearby, and they and many of the neighbors had been invited to share in the fun. Normally, since it was July, the tables would have been erected outside, so that everyone could enjoy the shade and the cool breezes, but it had been raining on and off for the past few days. It wasn't raining that afternoon, but the skies were heavy with threatening dark clouds, so the festivities were to be held indoors. Fortunately, Aunt Hannah's farmhouse was large and inviting.

After letting her parents out of the buggy and watching them cross the yard to the house, she drove the buggy over to the hitching post near the barn. As she was climbing down, Gideon appeared out of nowhere.

"You're late. I've been waiting for you," he said, offering his hand as she jumped down. "We'll be eating soon."

After she got down, he stood there. Close. She could have stepped around him, but instead, she stood there. Maybe to prove that her mother didn't rule her every action. Her *mam*'s suspicions about her and Gideon were unfounded. He *did* like her, she was certain of that, but not the way her mother had accused, in their kitchen that afternoon. Gideon liked her the same way he liked Ellie—as a friend. Not that it would have mattered if he liked her any other way. Strawberries would ripen in December before her mother and father would agree to allow her to court a penniless hired hand.

"We've been here for nearly an hour," Gideon said, still looming over her with that foolish grin on his face.

She moved the small brown-paper-wrapped birthday gift from one hand to the other. They *were* late. She'd wanted to come sooner to help Aunt Hannah get ready for supper. And she would have been there before Sara and her household if she and her mother hadn't had a disagreement over Gideon, but she wasn't about to tell him that. Her mother had asked how things were going with Andy and if she thought he would ask to walk out with her. Addy hadn't wanted to discuss Andy because she didn't know how she felt about him yet, but, as always, her mother was insistent.

"The trouble with you is that you spend too much time with that hired hand," her *mam* had said. "I don't know what Sara can be thinking. Having him there around her young women."

Every word of their conversation played over in Addy's head. "And what's wrong with Gideon? Sara's supposed to be finding him a wife." *That's why she's called a match-maker,* she had wanted to say. Of course she would have never been so rude.

"What's *wrong* with him? What's *right* with him? Gideon Esch has nothing, not a horse, not a buggy, not even a trade, so far as we know. He couldn't possibly support a wife. It's your duty to your father and me to marry a substantial man, a husband with land or a business like that butcher you turned your nose up at. You've let all this running around to ball games and singings go to your head. You can't afford to be so picky, daughter. It's foolish of Sara to put such notions in your head."

Addy hadn't answered back, although she had plenty on the tip of her tongue. Almost thirty or not, she wasn't brought up to show disrespect to her mother. Instead, she'd fled to her room and stayed there until her father had called her down an hour later. "Whatever fuss you and your mother have had, you owe it to her to apologize. Now, do your duty to your mother, and let's go to your aunt's and enjoy the celebration. Your mother wants only the best for you."

"I'll tie up for you." Gideon broke into her thoughts.

Gideon was standing closer to her than was proper. How they were with each other at work at Sara's was one thing, but now they were in public. What if someone should see? The yard was empty now. Everyone seemed to be inside, but someone could walk around the buggy at any second.

"Are you afraid I'll miss out on supper?" Addy said lightly, trying to ease the tension between them with humor. She passed him the reins, and he moved away from her. "There will be plenty of food. Aunt Hannah has eight daughters, all good cooks. Well..." She chuckled. "Almost all. Miriam is—" She broke off as a sudden curtain of cold rain splattered over her face and arms. *"Ach!"* she exclaimed. "David's gift! The paper will be soaked."

Securing the horse to the hitching post, Gideon grabbed her hand and took off toward the house. She had no choice but to follow, and she found herself laughing with him by the time they reached the shelter of the back porch.

Her cousin Rebecca pushed open the kitchen door and waited for them. If she noticed Gideon holding Addy's hand, she didn't let on. Addy pulled away from Gideon, running up the porch steps in front of him.

"Addy! It's good to see you." Rebecca kissed her cheek. "You can put that over there." She motioned inside to a table bearing a stack of wrapped gifts, and Addy added hers to the pile. "It's a penknife. David will probably get more than one, but it was the best idea I could come up with."

"I'm sure he'll love it, if Susanna will let him play with it." Rebecca chuckled. "I'm afraid my sister is overprotective where her husband is concerned." She smiled at Gideon. "Sara still hasn't found you a wife, I hear."

They all walked into the house.

"Not yet." Gideon grinned.

"Someone's been asking for you." Rebecca glanced toward the interior of the house. "Andy Mast."

"He's looking for me?" Gideon asked.

Rebecca laughed. "*Ne*, not you, Gideon. Addy."

Addy didn't notice Gideon's scowl. "I didn't know Andy was part of the family," he said. "I thought it was just family coming."

"Well," Rebecca explained, "he's a distant

relative of Anna's Samuel. Samuel's a Mast, but I believe Sara asked my mother to include Andy." She smiled. "I think he's sweet on you, Dorcas. Sorry." She shook her head. "*Addy* really *does* suit you better, cousin. I like it."

"Me, too," Addy admitted. She returned her cousin's smile. She liked Rebecca. She was closer in age to Rebecca's older sisters, but she and Rebecca had always hit it off. And the fact that Rebecca had married Caleb, the man who'd shown real interest in courting her, or that Rebecca and Caleb already had a baby, didn't matter. Despite her *mam*'s dire predictions, Addy had never felt a twinge of jealousy. The preacher had been no more right for her than the butcher. Maybe her mother was right. Maybe she *was* picky.

The ringing of a small iron triangle gave notice that the meal was served, so Addy, Gideon and Rebecca made their way through the crowded kitchen. Several tables stretched across the spacious room, and Addy could see others in the hall and front room. Friends and relatives called greetings to Addy, as if they hadn't all seen each other at worship last Sunday.

"Everyone find a seat," Aunt Hannah announced. "Anywhere you like. We're so happy that you could all be here on David's special day."

Everyone clapped and called words of congratulation, and David, seated beside Susanna at the largest table, turned raspberry-red with pleasure. As usual, David was wearing a paper crown from an English fast-food place, but if Gideon noticed, he wisely kept his observation to himself.

"It's his birthday!" Susanna shouted. "And we're going to have cake."

"Addy! Here's a spot." Andy Mast stood and waved to Addy. There was one place vacant, directly across from Andy, and no other chairs empty at the table.

"I see some places open in the front room," Gideon said, but Andy was still motioning to her.

"You go ahead," Addy told Gideon. "I'll sit here with my cousins."

"Andy's a cousin, now, is he?"

Gideon's remark, as he walked away, made Addy stiffen. What was wrong with him? She wasn't talking about Andy. Miriam and Miriam's half sister, Grace, were seated on either side of her.

Andy made eye contact with her and grinned. "I think someone is put out. Maybe he wishes there was more room here, *ya*?"

Addy nodded. She liked Andy. He was fun, and he wasn't that much younger than she was. Maybe they would make a good couple. As her *mam* liked to say, Andy Mast had "prospects." His father had a growing lawn furniture business, and Andy worked alongside him. They shipped outdoor pieces as far away as New England. Andy was just telling her the other day that he was thinking of raising free-range turkeys for the English Thanksgiving market. Andy was ambitious and a faithful member of his church.

He'd make someone a good husband. Why not her?

Andy kept up a steady conversation with Addy and the others at the table through the meal. He was never pushy or obnoxious, and he always had a smile or a joke ready when there was a lull in the conversation. Addy enjoyed the chicken and dumplings, the roast beef and the other dishes her aunt and cousins had prepared. It was always enjoyable to eat someone else's cooking.

After everyone was finished eating, the men and boys went outside to the barn, while the women cleared away the tables and washed the dishes. Later, David would open his gifts, and cake would be served with coffee, iced tea and a nonalcoholic punch. Susanna loved the red punch with sweet cherries floating in it. Addy didn't know exactly what went into it; the Yoder girls wouldn't tell, but everyone raved about it.

It was the punch that caused Addy's disaster. She, Rebecca, Ellie and the other young women were serving dessert to the men and children. Addy had a brimming pitcher of punch, and Ellie was coming behind her with a tray of glasses. Since it had stopped raining, some of the men were standing in the backyard. Again, Andy caught sight of her first and shouted to her. "Addy! Over here!" He, Thomas and Gideon had found a dry spot under the overhanging roof that jutted out from Albert's tool shed. But as she approached, Addy sensed that Andy and Gideon seemed to be having a disagreement over something. They were talking in low voices, but both sounded annoyed.

"What's going on?" she asked as she reached them. "You aren't—" What they were or were not doing would never be clear to Addy, because Andy abruptly gave Gideon a push. Gideon stumbled back into her.

Addy yelped as the pitcher of punch splashed over the bodice of her light green dress, soaking the waist and trailing big stains down the skirt. *"Ne!"* She exhaled as she stared down at the mess. The cherry juice would ruin her dress if she didn't wash it out immediately. It might be a total loss no matter what she did. She clutched at the half-empty pitcher and tried not to let her distress show.

"See what you did?" Gideon gave Andy a push.

"Enough of that!" Thomas wrapped his arms around Andy and steered him away from Gideon. "Let's take a walk." Thomas hustled a protesting Andy around the corner of the building and out of sight.

Ellie came from behind Addy and took the pitcher of punch out of her hands. "You'll want to wash that quick," she advised.

"Are you all right, Addy?" Gideon demanded. "That fool—"

"That fool?" Addy felt heat flush her cheeks as she turned on him. "I think there are two woodenheads here tonight. What's wrong with you? Have you lost what good sense you ever had to behave so? To lay hands on one another in anger?"

"He started it," Gideon protested. "He pushed me first."

"He pushed you first? What were you arguing over?" She was trembling with anger now. "Look at my dress. Look at me. Now I've got to go home and change out of it before it's ruined."

"I'm sorry. I'll take you," he said, immediately contrite. "In Sara's buggy. Let me drive you."

"Ride with you? Not if I had to walk home ten miles in the rain!" She turned and strode away into the growing twilight. As she did, thunder rumbled in the west.

"You're not walking home alone," Gideon said, following her and catching her by the arm. "Just let me drive you to your house. Or I'll walk with you."

"Stay away from me. You started this. You're jealous of Andy because he wants to walk out with me. No matter who it is, you find fault with them," Addy sputtered. "First Joseph, then the butcher. You did everything you could at Sara's dinner to show him up for a pompous…a pompous…fuddy-duddy."

"He *was* a pompous fuddy-duddy."

Addy was vaguely aware that Ellie was right behind Gideon and could hear every word, but she didn't care. Angry accusations bubbled up inside her, and when she opened her mouth, she couldn't hold them back. "You know what?" She started walking again. Fast. "The trouble with you, Gideon Esch, is that you like me yourself. And you're too much of a coward to admit it!"

"*Ne!* That's not it," he protested, following after her. "I'm just… I'm looking out for you. You deserve better than Andy Mast, who isn't old enough to grow a proper beard."

"At least he's man enough to court a woman!"

That stopped him short in his shoes. "Addy…"

"Addy, nothing." She stopped and turned back to him. "If you'd be honest with yourself, you'd know that I'm speaking the truth."

She started walking again; suddenly, her eyes were stinging. She was afraid she was going to cry. "I'm going home."

"You can't go home by yourself. Let me go with—"

"I'll go with her," Ellie said, following Addy. "I think the two of you have said quite enough to each other for one night."

"But it's going to rain," Gideon protested after her.

"Good," Ellie called over her shoulder. "Because if anyone needs cooling off, both of you do."

Chapter Eleven

Saturday morning, Gideon guided Sara's mule, Jasper, close to the front door of Byler's Country Store. "Is this rain ever going to let up?" he wondered aloud, not really expecting Sara or Ellie, who were sitting next to him, to answer.

"When the Lord wills it," Sara said cheerfully.

Rolling to a halt, he wrapped the reins around a bar on the dashboard and got down to help Sara out of the buggy. "Careful," he warned, offering his hand. "Watch out for that puddle."

"*Danke.*" Once she was on the pavement,

her skirts in proper order, she turned around and looked up. "You coming, Ellie?"

"I'll walk in with Gideon," Ellie said. "I have an umbrella. You go on ahead. I'll find you inside."

As Gideon got back into the buggy, Ellie slid a proper distance away from him on the bench seat. He drove past a line of automobiles in search of a place at the hitching rack at the east end of the building. Despite the downpour, the parking lot was crowded. Saturdays were always busy at Byler's, with both Amish and Englishers doing their shopping. Four other buggies stood waiting for their occupants, the horses' hides soaked. Jasper disliked rain. The mule's ears were flattened against his big head, and he trudged along as though pulling a heavy load instead of the light carriage with only two passengers.

Ellie waved to another family from their church district that was just leaving. "It's really coming down. Poor Jasper. Maybe we should have waited until afternoon. It will be a mess getting our groceries in."

"I'll bring the buggy back up to the door to load them," he told her. "And don't worry about Jasper. The rain's warm enough. He'll be fine."

A pickup backed up in front of them, and Gideon reined the mule in until the vehicle was out of the way. Two more English women pushing carts crossed in front of Jasper. Gideon sighed. Saturdays there were always crazy. He didn't know why Sara was always set on doing her dealing on the busiest day of the week.

Truth was that he wasn't in the mood for shopping or crowds. He couldn't stop rehashing his and Addy's exchange the previous night. The way she'd stomped off across the field had really ticked him off. She'd been unreasonable. The disagreement with Andy hadn't been a big deal; he'd apologized and shook hands with him twenty minutes later. *After* he'd apologized to Addy for spilling the drink. After he'd watched her stomp off.

He glanced at Ellie as he eased into a spot at the end of the row of horses and buggies.

He needed to talk to someone, but didn't want to explain the situation to either Joseph or Sara. Ellie had been there; she'd heard the words out of Addy's mouth. Maybe she'd have some insight.

He glanced at Ellie. "Why would Addy say such things to me? I know she was upset over the punch spilling on her dress, but that was an accident. I didn't mean it. Neither did Andy."

Ellie turned to face him, her eyes narrowed. "*Ne*, you didn't mean it, but if you and Andy hadn't been acting like schoolyard children, it wouldn't have happened, would it?"

For a second, he couldn't think of what to say. That wasn't the reaction he'd expected from Ellie. She was usually so sensible.

"What were you two talking about that made you think you needed to lay hands on each other?" she asked. But she didn't give him a chance to answer. "I'll bet it was about Addy."

He thought about saying it wasn't, but Ellie

was a perceptive woman. And he wasn't a liar. He exhaled loudly, frustrated. "They're not right for each other, Andy and Addy. I mean, try to say that a couple of times. Addy and Andy. Andy and Addy."

Ellie arched her eyebrows.

"I'm just trying to look out for her," Gideon explained. "She's like a sister to me. You can see that, can't you?"

Ellie folded her arms over her chest and glared. "What I see is that you were completely in the wrong last night."

"Me?"

"*Ya*, you."

"What about Andy? He pushed me first."

"All right. So you're both woodenheads."

"But you heard what Addy said." He fingered the leather reins in his hands. "She called me a coward. She said that I was jealous of Andy and finding fault with him and Nathan King because I like her myself. So my question to you is, when have I ever—"

"Gideon Esch, listen to what you're saying." She shook a stubby finger at him.

"You're so caught up in your own invention of who you are and what you want out of life that you don't know your own feelings. Either you can't see or you refuse to be honest with yourself."

Ellie must have realized his astonishment at her reaction because she glanced down at her accusing finger, blushed and tucked it behind her. "I've tried to hold my tongue and stay out of it. Sara asked me to let it be and let the two of you work this out, but you asked for my opinion, and I'm giving it. If you believe that you act toward Addy as if she were one of your sisters, you need to drop down on your knees and pray for the Lord to show you what's really in your heart."

Gideon was surprised to hear that Sara and Ellie had been talking about him and Addy. What had Sara meant, saying he and Addy needed to "work things out"? Now he was more confused than ever.

He jumped down off the buggy bench and fastened the tie rope to the hitching rack.

Paying no heed to the rain drenching his clothing, he splashed through the puddles back to the buggy and climbed back in.

"So what you're saying here is that you're taking her side in this?" he asked.

"There isn't any side. I care about both of you."

He stared out through the wet windshield at Jasper's back. He didn't know what to say. What to think. Could there be truth in what Ellie was saying? Which would mean there was truth in Addy's accusation.

"You asked me what I think. I think you act like a man smitten, Gideon. Yet you…" Ellie sighed in exasperation. "If you're interested in Addy, you'd better step up and tell her so. If you're not, then it isn't fair to keep her from finding a husband. She cares what you think. And if you don't want her for your wife, you need to stop throwing obstacles in the way of men who might."

"Aren't you going to be late for work?" Monday morning, Addy's father threw the lever that set the arms of the windmill in motion. The gears ground and clattered and the wind power drew water from the well and sent it gushing down the overhead pipe and into the pig trough.

Addy had already carried kitchen scraps to the hogs, milked the cow and fed the chickens. She'd also cleaned up and washed the breakfast dishes. Now she was headed toward the garden with a basket on her arm. She stopped and looked at her father, unsure of what to say. She couldn't lie to him, but she didn't want to tell him the whole truth, either. *"Ya,"* she said reluctantly. "But I'm not sure I should go this morning. My stomach is a little *ryenich*. Sour."

He shielded his eyes from the sun with a tanned hand. "You should go if Sara's expecting you. If you don't, she may decide to hire someone else, and where else would you find a job? If you don't save your wages, you'll have nothing for your bride box."

Addy swallowed hard and forced a half smile. Her *dat* was right. She needed the job at Sara's. And she loved it there, loved her time with Ellie and Sara, Gideon and Joseph. But how could she face Gideon after what she'd said to him at David's birthday party? She hadn't seen him since then. The previous day had been a visiting Sunday, and she'd spent the day with her parents going to the homes of several elderly folks in Seven Poplars.

"You go," her father said. "It's a fine day. By the time you get there, you will have walked off your stomachache."

So Addy went, though not gladly. Each step from her father's house to Sara's kitchen was like going to her own funeral. What if her quarrel with Gideon ruined her relationship with Ellie and Sara, too? For the first time in her life, she had friends, and she was popular at young people's gatherings. Would that all end now because of her own stubbornness?

When Addy arrived at Sara's place, she was surprised to find Jasper missing from the field, the buggy gone and the house quiet. Ellie was alone in the kitchen, making jam.

"Sara and Gideon have gone for the day," Ellie said as Addy came into the kitchen. "Off to meet with some prospective families. Sara didn't say who." She used a pot holder to pull the kettle off the heat, dried her hands on a towel and came to put her arms out to her. "It's good to see you, Addy."

Addy stooped to accept Ellie's hug.

"What's wrong?" Ellie asked. "You look like you just lost your best friend."

"Oh, Ellie, I was such a fool." Releasing her, she stood up. "You heard what I said to Gideon. I accused him of liking me. How can I ever face him again?"

"Sit down," Ellie ordered. "I'll put a pot of tea on. Nothing ever seems as bad over a cup of tea. And no tears. We'll figure this out."

Addy sniffed and dropped into a chair. "No tears," she repeated. Then she covered her face with her hands. "I'm so embarrassed. I wouldn't blame him if he told people what

I said to him, but...I'll be the joke of the county if anyone finds out."

Ellie filled the teakettle with water. "Time somebody put him in his place. He's too sure of himself, all puffed up with his own self-importance. I think he had it coming." She carried her stool over to the cabinet and climbed onto it to get down a canister of tea leaves. "Assam or Earl Grey?"

"Either one."

Ellie held up both tins. "You pick. You're the one having the crisis." Addy motioned to the Earl Grey, and when the water boiled, Ellie made the tea and brought it to the table.

"I'm so sorry for what I said, Ellie. I wish I could take it back." She watched Ellie climb up into her chair. "Should I apologize? What should I do?"

Ellie poured tea into the pretty porcelain cups with the roses on the side. "It seems to me that Gideon should be apologizing to you, considering the trouble he's caused—finding fault with every man Sara looks at for you."

"*Ya*, he did do that, but he said it was because we're friends, and he only wanted what's best for me. That has to be it." She stirred a spoon of sugar in her cup, then slowly added another...and another.

"Enough sugar." Ellie grabbed the sugar bowl. "Next we'll have to find a dentist because you'll rot all your teeth."

"It's fine." She took a sip, gasped at how sweet it was and clapped a hand over her mouth.

"*Ya*, fine." Ellie chuckled, carried the cup to the sink, dumped it and poured another cup for her.

"*Danke.*" She glanced at Ellie. "I still can't believe I said such a thing. How silly it must have sounded. Gideon is handsome, hardworking, pleasant...a real catch. There's no way he could be interested in a beanpole with a face like mine. *Mam* says a plain face is an asset to a woman, but I know very well—"

"Stop it, Addy. Listen to yourself. You sound like the old Dorcas. Have you learned nothing from Sara since you've been here? Gideon doesn't think you're plain."

"He doesn't?" She looked up from her teacup. "How do you know?"

"He told me so himself. He thinks you have pretty eyes. And a nice smile. And he really likes that you're so smart. And that you speak your mind."

"He does?" Addy knew her mouth must have been hanging open, making her look neither pretty nor smart.

Ellie toyed with the handle of her cup. "You know what I think," she said slowly, looking as if she were going over things in her mind. "I think you're right. I think he *does* like you and furthermore—" she met Addy's gaze "—I think you like him. Both of you are just too pigheaded to know it."

A small eddy of joy swirled in the pit of Addy's stomach, and for a second, she found it hard to catch her breath. But then the reality of their situation settled heavily on her shoulders. She stared at Ellie across the table. "What if I do like him? And what if, by some crazy chance, he likes me? My parents would never allow us to marry. You heard him. His family is so poor, they sell sausage to their neighbors to make ends meet. Gideon could never afford Sara's fee. It's hopeless."

Ellie's small hand covered hers. "Maybe it is, and maybe it isn't," she said in her high, sweet voice. "Who knows what God's plan is for any of us? I'm certainly proof of that. I always wanted to be independent, to prove that I could take care of myself as well as any average-size woman. I tried my best, but no school board would hire me. My parents kept urging me to marry, marry anyone who would take me off their hands. I prayed so hard, and when I began to believe that the Lord didn't hear me, Sara invited me here to Seven Poplars. She offered me a home with her, and she found me a job teaching school." Ellie's pretty red-cheeked face glowed with an inner light. "If my dreams can come true, maybe yours can, too. Have faith, Addy. Put your trust in Him."

* * *

Gideon spent Monday with Sara, driving her first to Dover to the bank, and then different homes to interview prospective matches. At the third farm, farthest away, Sara interviewed a middle-aged widow who was seeking a second husband. She had one child still at home, and two living nearby. She was hoping Sara could help her to arrange a marriage with a man who would be willing to come to Delaware, rather than her having to move away and be separated from her two married daughters. Sara was well pleased with the woman and promised to see what she could do.

Gideon had remained outside at each stop until he was invited inside. Sara took her position as matchmaker seriously, and it was only natural that her clients expected privacy when financial compensation was discussed. Even though part of the conversations were private, he still ended up being invited in at the first potential client's for dinner, for coffee and pound cake at the second and finally for a light supper with the widow and her son.

The time Gideon spent waiting for Sara gave him the solitude to think about Addy. As his hands were busy grooming Jasper, braiding a rope halter or whittling, he kept mulling over what she had said...and what Ellie had said. And he came to the conclusion that what he really needed to do was talk to Addy.

When they arrived home at Sara's, Gideon unhitched Jasper, fed and watered him and tended to the evening chores. Since they'd arrived later than evening milking time, Ellie had milked the cow. He rushed through what remained, returned to the bunkhouse he shared with Joseph, shaved and changed into a clean shirt. Then, hoping that it wasn't too late to go visiting, he jogged across the fields to Addy's house.

To Gideon's disappointment, it was full dark by the time he got there. No lights glowed in the downstairs windows. The entire house was dark except for a single lamp glowing upstairs in one of the bedrooms. *Whose room is that?* he wondered. He knew that Addy lived alone with her mother and father. Would it be too much to hope that it was Addy who was still awake?

Gideon stared at the window. Rationally, he knew that he should go home and wait for the next morning. He could draw Addy aside when she came to work, find a quiet spot to tell her that he truly was sorry for the trouble he'd caused. He would ask her to find it in her heart to forgive, not just his behavior with Andy, but also his actions toward her over the past few weeks. She was too important to him to have his foolishness come between them.

But he was afraid that if he waited, he'd lose his nerve. And how could he sleep with this on his mind? What if Addy was still awake because she still felt hurt at what he'd said? What if she really cared for Andy and she believed that he had ruined her chances with the young man? No, what had to be done had to be done now, before it was too late.

On a whim, Gideon stooped and picked up a handful of small pebbles from the driveway. He moved closer to the house and tossed a single stone at the upstairs window. It was too dark for anyone to see him from the second floor. If Addy's mother or father came to the window, he'd just stand there in the shadows until they decided a bird or an insect had hit the pane. He waited.

Nothing. Seconds ticked by and then a minute. He tossed another stone, a little harder this time. It pinged against the upper glass of the open window.

Throwing pebbles against girls' windows was tricky. Once, he'd thrown too hard and broken a windowpane. Luckily, the brother of the girl whose attention he'd been trying to attract was one of his good chums. They'd managed to replace the broken pane without the parents' knowledge. His friends, the *maedle* included, had all thought it a great joke.

Tonight, Gideon didn't feel like laughing. He threw one more pebble; this one went *in* the window. Again, he waited. Nothing.

He was just about to turn away, when Addy appeared in the window. She had something between her fingers. His pebble, he guessed.

She didn't speak; she just stood there, her graceful form illuminated by the soft yellow glow of a kerosene lamp. She leaned out over the sill, and her long brown hair fell loose around her shoulders. Gideon's mouth went suddenly dry, as a wave of tenderness washed over him. Addy was dressed for bed in a long white nightgown, and he was struck by her loveliness.

"Is someone there?" she called, not apprehensive, but curious.

Addy... She always kept him guessing. However he thought she would, she always behaved differently.

"It's Gideon," he answered. He kept his voice low, hoping it wouldn't carry. He didn't want to wake her parents.

"What are you doing out there?" She sounded surprised, but not angry. He hoped she wasn't still angry with him.

"I know it's too late to come visiting, but I

had to talk to you tonight." He moved closer. She dropped to her knees in the low window and leaned on the sill. It was quiet; not a breeze stirred the leaves of the maple tree beside the house. "Can you come down?"

"*Ne*, my mother and father's room is near the stairs. She sleeps fitfully. She'd hear me and ask where I'm going."

He took comfort in the way she spoke, not insisting that he go, only explaining why she couldn't come out. He moved back from the edge of the building, scanning the roofline. The roof of an addition, probably the kitchen, was nearly flat. He could reach it if he climbed the tree, and it ran right under Addy's window. He considered if going onto the roof might compromise her reputation. But he wasn't going into her bedroom, just meeting her on the roof.

"You could climb up," Addy whispered.

"What?" He must have heard wrong. How had she guessed what he'd been thinking?

"Climb the tree. I used to do it all the time.

Drop onto the kitchen roof and I'll come out there."

He didn't ask why she was offering to do such an outrageous thing. He leaped for the bottom branch of the maple tree and pulled himself up from one limb to another, finally reaching the height of the flat roof and swinging over. Addy was stepping through the open window when he reached her. She had put a robe on over her nightgown.

"Give me your hand," he said, and a jolt of excitement ran through him as her fingers closed tightly around his.

Overhead, the clouds parted, and moonlight shone through, shining on Addy's face. Gideon wondered how he'd ever believed she was plain. He wanted to touch her hair, but he was afraid to frighten her by being too bold. He'd never seen a woman's hair down, other than his mother's or his sisters', and he thought it was the most beautiful thing he'd ever seen.

Addy unwound her hand from his and tightened the tie of her robe. It was white, like her nightgown, thick enough for decency, but thin enough that he could make out her shape beneath it. A graceful shape.

He could sense her nervousness. Now that she'd joined him on the roof, he could see that she was hesitant about her decision.

"You can trust me," he said sincerely. "I'd never do anything to harm you."

"But you have," she said. Her voice was soft, almost a whisper. "What you and Andy—"

He cut her off. "That was wrong. *I* was wrong."

"I should go in."

"*Ne*, Addy, please, don't go." The warm night air, the moonlight, the sweet smell of honeysuckle, the chirp of crickets—he didn't want this small piece of happiness to end. "Can't we just sit here and talk…for a few minutes?" He dropped down to sit.

"Maybe…just for a little while," she conceded.

He took a deep breath, trying to remember what he had intended to say, then patted the place beside him. "I was trying to drive off your suitors." He exhaled. "I'm sorry, Addy. It was wrong of me."

She sat beside him. Close, but not too close.

Somewhere, far off on another farm, a dog barked; the sound was followed by more barking. More dogs.

"Maybe a fox after somebody's chickens," he said. When he looked at her, he found that she was already looking at him.

Gideon felt a sudden impulse to put his arm around Addy, to tell her that he wanted to stand before the bishop with her. He wanted to make her his own, to protect her and take care of her. He had heard people speak of their life flashing before them, and he suddenly understood.

He could see them laughing together at the breakfast table…walking to Sunday services together…raising a family and making a home. He sucked in a deep breath and then another. He felt so lighthearted that it seemed he would rise in the air and float off the roof. Happiness filled him.

Why hadn't he realized how special she was the morning she'd tumbled off the broken stile steps and into the briars? She'd felt so good in his arms. He'd never met anyone like her, and he'd been too dumb to realize that she was what he'd been looking for all along...maybe what God had intended from the beginning.

"Addy...Addy," he said, and he began to chuckle. "I've been such a fool."

Chapter Twelve

Addy shivered, almost too excited to speak. Nothing like this had ever happened to her before. Gideon coming to her house in the darkness, throwing pebbles at her window, climbing her special tree to sit with her under the moonlight—it was so romantic, like something out of a book.

And now Gideon had admitted that she'd been right when she'd accused him of liking her himself. The thought that a man like Gideon could be attracted to her—Dorcas Coblentz—was almost too much to accept. But it hadn't happened to Dorcas, because she wasn't Dorcas anymore; she was Addy.

And Addy was someone who could win at games, lead the singing and was a popular girl that other people wanted to be with.

Gideon took her hand, and she found herself smiling at him. His hand was big and warm, and his touch sent shivers of pleasure up her arm. He was still talking.

"…meet with your father tomorrow and ask permission to court you."

Addy blinked. Gideon wanted to *court* her? The enormity of that settled over her. Gideon was saying that he wanted to *marry* her. Tears gathered behind her eyelids, and all her joy was drowned in a flood of reality.

Addy couldn't marry Gideon.

It didn't matter that she cared for him as she'd never cared for another young man… that she might even love him. Her parents would never approve. He had no skills, no land, no money. If they were to wed, they would be worse off than her mother and father. For the rest of their lives, they'd be hired help, living in someone else's home, working for wages with little to spare to provide for her aging parents.

Her mother would never agree to the marriage. She'd made it clear when they'd hired Sara that she was looking for someone who could provide a better home than Addy's father had. Her mother wasn't even willing to pay the matchmaker's fee; that would be up to Addy's husband-to-be's family.

If she went to her father and explained how she and Gideon cared for each other and asked for his blessing, it would do no good. Her father would hem and haw and promise to think on the matter, but in the end, he would do what her *mam* wanted, because it had always been that way. She closed her eyes against her tears. It was her *duty* to take care of her parents in their old age. It was her duty to marry a man who could help her take care of her parents.

But how could she tell Gideon that he couldn't court her because he was poor? How could she shame him so?

She tried to think.

It would be kinder to let him down easily, wouldn't it? To give some other reason…

Addy pulled her hand away from his and bit down on her lower lip. "*Ne*, Gideon, I…I'm sorry if I made you think… I don't want to walk out with you," she blurted. She suddenly felt sick.

"I… What? You don't?"

The hurt in his voice made her choke up. "You know I like you," she said, "but I don't think of you *that* way. You're a friend, more like a brother. I couldn't—"

"But I thought…"

She stared straight ahead, into the branches of the tree he had climbed to come to her, willing herself not to cry. "You thought wrong."

He stammered something, apologized and rose to his feet. "Addy…is there any chance that you could change your mind?" he asked.

"I don't think so, Gideon. It's better this way." She stared straight ahead, afraid that if she looked at him, he might know she wasn't being truthful. "Better we remain friends."

He climbed back down the tree, leaving her alone on the roof beneath the moon and scattered stars. She stared up, dashing away the tears that slid down her cheeks.

She tried to pray, but the words wouldn't come. God had answered her prayers. He'd sent her the man she'd dreamed about all her life, and she'd refused him over a silly thing like money. She'd told him that she wanted to remain his friend, but she knew that would never happen. Truthfully, Gideon would probably never be her friend again. She'd lost her one chance, and she must be content in surrendering all hope for her own personal happiness. She would have to take solace in doing what was right, no matter how much she had to sacrifice. Wasn't that what the bishop preached?

The following week was difficult for Addy; it was all she could do to make herself go to work at Sara's. She was busy, though, which helped take her mind off her broken heart. There was housecleaning to be done, and because it was late July and crops were ripening, there was plenty of picking and canning to do.

Addy saw Gideon coming and going, but they both made a point not to be in the same place at the same time, if they could help it. When they *did* run into each other, in the kitchen or in the yard, they both attempted to pretend that nothing had happened between them, but that had been a dismal failure. Instead of their usual banter, their conversations had been awkward and uncomfortable. For both of them. If Ellie or Sara noticed anything going on between Addy and Gideon, they didn't mention it.

The same week, Aunt Hannah's orchard produced a bumper peach crop. She always offered to let Addy's family pick as many as they liked, so Addy's mother insisted they go pick peaches two afternoons in a row, right after work.

On Wednesday, the second day of peach-picking, Addy and her mother worked side by side. Each of them wore a special kind of

apron with one deep pocket across the front
for putting peaches in. Because peaches were
fragile and easy to bruise, it was important
to handle each piece of fruit carefully and
not to pile too many on top of each other.

"I haven't talked with Sara this week."
Addy's mother eyed her. "Any new prospects? With the fair starting, there must be
boys in town looking for girls."

Addy reached up and picked a big, fat,
ripe peach. When she plucked it from the
branch, she could smell the sweet aroma of
the fruit. Ordinarily, she loved the smell of
ripe peaches, but today, she couldn't even
appreciate it, she was feeling so down.

"Your father was disappointed the butcher
didn't suit." Her mother looked right at her.
Addy kept picking. "It would have been nice
to have a butcher in the family. All the pork
chops your father could eat."

Right now, Addy couldn't stand the thought
of meeting another man at Sara's dinner table
or letting another boy walk her home from a
singing. Every time she thought about meet-

ing another of Sara's prospects, she was reminded of what she and Gideon might have had together. Of what she was afraid she would never have with someone else.

"What was wrong with the butcher?" her mother pressed when Addy didn't answer. "He has a big house and a nice shop. Clean for a butcher. And plenty of money, I hear."

"A man's money is all you talk about," Addy responded, trying to keep the bitterness out of her voice. She'd heard bitterness from her mother her whole life, and she didn't want to be that person. Not ever. She added another peach to her apron. "What does it matter how much money a man makes, if he has a good heart?"

Her mother sniffed and began to slowly empty her apron pocket into a half-bushel basket. When the six they had brought were full, Addy would load them in the back of the wagon to take home. She'd stay up late into the night to peel and cut and process the peaches so they could go into the Ball jars and be preserved to be eaten that winter.

"You wouldn't ask that if you'd ever not had the money to put boots on your children in winter, or watched a calf die because you couldn't afford the price of the veterinarian."

Addy closed her eyes for a moment. Her head understood what her mother was saying, but her *heart*... "I see what you're saying, but I'm just asking, *Mam*. What if I were to meet someone special, someone I felt was right for me, and he wasn't financially well-off?"

"That's why you pick and choose who you walk out with, daughter." She shook her head, walking back toward the peach tree they were picking from. "That's why I asked Sara to help us. So you have the right kinds of boys to pick from."

Addy focused on a peach just above her head, afraid that if she met her mother's gaze, her mother might suspect whom she was talking about. She knew she shouldn't say any more. The matter was settled. But she couldn't help herself. "But what if I *did* meet a poor boy, and I wanted to marry him?"

"Then you'd have to think long and hard about your duty to us," her mother said, taking a big bite out of a peach she'd just picked. "Because without you, your father and I will end up living on your Aunt Hannah's leavings."

A week later, Sara hired a driver to take a group of young men and women, including Ellie, Thomas and Gideon, to the fair. Addy had wanted to go with them, but her mother and father had been invited to go with Bishop Atlee, his wife and another older couple. When she'd mentioned going with Sara, her mother wouldn't have it, insisting it was important they go as a family with the bishop.

And so, reluctantly, Addy had accompanied the bishop's party in his rented van, with a driver so elderly and cautious that, although they left the house at eight sharp, it was 10:00 a.m. by the time they paid admission and entered the main gate. With her parents, Addy made the familiar rounds of the cow barns, the poultry area and the 4-H exhibits.

The fair in Harrington was the same as it had always been: hot, noisy and crowded with families and people of all ages who'd come to enjoy themselves. Music drifted from the midway, where a giant Ferris wheel, a Tilt-a-Whirl, a merry-go-round and a dozen other rides had been erected on the fairgrounds. But that was not an area condoned by Addy's parents or any other Amish elder. Carnival rides, cork-gun-shooting booths, guess-your-weight shills, baseball throws and ring tosses were worldly entertainment for Englishers. But that didn't mean that Addy didn't have a secret wish to see for herself what the excitement was all about.

By noon, the original group had split up, with Bishop Atlee and his wife going in one direction, the Troyers in another and the Coblentzes in another. Once Addy's father had inspected the second horse barn and the swine sheds, he was anxious to go on to inspect the sheep and goats. Her mother objected, insisting that she and Addy had been waiting to visit the horticulture exhibit.

By then, Addy was out of patience. "Actually, I'd rather go to the conservation building," she ventured. "Maybe we could each go—"

"Nonsense." Her mother fanned her face with a paper fan advertising a funeral home. "We're a family. We came together to enjoy the day, and we'll remain together. No use in you looking at sheep, Reuben." She waved her fan at him for emphasis. "It's not as though you can afford to buy any. Now, let's go to see the flower arrangements. The building is air-conditioned."

"Addy!" Her cousins, Rebecca and Susanna, waved and then crossed the street to join them. "I just saw Sara," Rebecca said. "She was so excited. She thinks that Ellie has a good chance to win with her elderberry custard pie entry. Judging is later this afternoon."

"The new schoolteacher made the pie," Susanna explained, loudly. "She's a little girl."

"I told you," Rebecca told her sister, "Ellie is a *little person*."

Susanna nodded. "She's little. So how can she be a teacher if she's not big?"

Rebecca smiled fondly at her. "Susanna and I are on our way to get funnel cakes. Do you want to join us, Addy?" Rebecca threw her a meaningful look.

Addy's mother frowned. "We were going to the flower displays."

"I'll catch up with you," Addy said, seizing the opportunity to escape with her cousins. "You know I love funnel cake." And before her mother could raise a protest that the sweet was overpriced, Addy hurried off with her cousins. *"Danke,"* she exclaimed.

At the end of the street, they turned the corner, and Gideon stepped out from behind an ice cream cart in front of her. "Can I interest you in a sundae on a stick?"

Addy stopped short and burst out laughing. Gideon looked so silly, standing there holding out a chocolate-covered frozen sundae with a cherry on the top. Addy glanced at

Rebecca and Susanna, who were both giggling. "You planned this, didn't you? Gideon put you up to it."

"Guilty," he said, and he handed the sundae on a stick to Susanna. "All my idea. Rebecca was just willing to help a boy out. I saw you with your mother and father, and I thought maybe you—"

"Maybe you'd like to get away for some fun," Rebecca finished for him. "We're going for that funnel cake. Enjoy yourself." Taking Susanna's hand, Rebecca walked away.

Addy didn't know what to do. Having Gideon meet her like this was exciting, but she knew it wasn't smart. She was doing her best to avoid him until her feelings for him eased. Now all those emotions rushed back, stronger than ever. "I shouldn't be here," she said hesitantly.

"Maybe this is exactly where you *should* be." He fixed her with those beautiful gray eyes, catching her gaze and holding it. "Rebecca told me that you like the merry-go-round. Would you like to ride it with me?"

She felt breathless. The heat, the crowds of people, everything and everyone seemed to grow dim around her. She could hear the blare of music from the midway, and the laughter and shrieks of people riding the rides. She knew it was the wrong thing to do, but all her life she'd loved the idea of a merry-go-round with the flashing lights, the pretty sounds and the painted animals. She'd never ridden a merry-go-round, never ridden the Ferris wheel or the Tilt-a-Whirl, but she'd wanted to. Just once, she wanted to experience the thrill of the forbidden world of the Englishers.

"You asked me if I wanted a sundae," she said. "But I didn't get it. You gave it to another girl."

"Susanna? A married woman," he corrected.

"Just the same, how do I know you'll really take me on the merry-go-round if I agree?"

He laughed. "I guess you'll have to trust me, Addy."

"My parents wouldn't approve."

"But what do *you* say? You can't always do what they tell you. You're a grown woman. You have a right to choose."

And I do, she thought. *I have a right to think for myself. I can honor my parents and my faith and still be my own person.* She wanted to ride the merry-go-round. If she said no, would she ever get the chance again?

"I'll go with you," she said boldly, "but only if you let me buy you lunch."

Gideon grinned. "You want to buy my lunch?"

"I'm hungry. *Mam* packed a cooler but I don't want the tuna salad I eat at my father's table every week. They say the Grange makes the best fried chicken and cole slaw at the fair. First lunch, and then you take me on the merry-go-round."

"And your parents? You won't get in trouble with them?"

It was her turn to laugh. "Probably. They'll worry if I don't meet them later."

"Not for long," he replied. "I told Rebecca

to tell them not to wait for you. That you were catching a ride home with friends."

"You were that sure I'd say yes?"

He laughed again. "*Ne*, not sure, but hopeful." He caught her hand. "Now, where's this Grange building with the good chicken?"

The Grange chicken was some of the best fried chicken that Gideon had ever eaten. He allowed Addy to pay for them both because it seemed so important that she do so. And he was rewarded by her animated features, her laughter and her obvious joy in the simple meal of cole slaw, fries, roll and chicken. The tent where the picnic tables had been set up was filled with people enjoying a hot midday meal in the comfort of air-conditioning and huge fans. He and Addy weren't the only Amish eating there, so they attracted few stares from the other fair-goers.

Gideon was again struck by how pretty Addy was in her lavender dress, her dark apron and black bonnet, with her prayer *kapp* peeking out beneath the deep brim. If only she would laugh more often, he thought. She looked younger today, her eyes sparkling, more girlish and vulnerable than he'd ever seen her. As he watched her, he was nearly overcome by his desire to make certain that Addy never lost that expression of wonder again.

Once they'd finished their meal, they ducked back outside into the hot afternoon sun and made their way toward the tinny Wurlitzer sounds of the carousel. The closer they got to it, the more animated Addy became. She was positively bouncing up and down as they stood in line to buy the tickets. When he reached the window, he glanced at her. "You're going to ride? You're sure? Not backing out on me, are you?"

After the night on her roof, after she'd told him she didn't want to walk out with him, he'd actually considered going home to Wisconsin. He couldn't believe he could have been mistaken about Addy's feelings for him. He certainly wasn't mistaken about his own; that had become plainer to him with each passing day. But it had also become obvious to him that Addy hadn't been happy. Not since the night on the roof. He suspected—hoped—that maybe she was having second thoughts. And that maybe he still had a chance with her.

Addy giggled and met his gaze "*Ne*, I'm not backing out. I do want to ride."

The merry-go-round wasn't as crowded as some of the rides, and they were able to get on after only a five-minute wait. "Which one do you want to ride?" he asked.

When she pointed to a glittering gold-and-white horse with a flowing mane and tail on the outer rim, he caught her by the waist and lifted her up.

She motioned to a striped black-and-orange tiger. "Aren't you going to ride?"

But he remained where he was, standing beside her, where he could sense every ounce of her excitement. And then the organ began to play, the gears groaned and the merry-go-round began to move. Onlookers waved and called out to their children and friends.

Laughing, Addy waved back and laughed merrily as the gold-and-white horse began to go up and down.

Gideon just watched Addy.

Chapter Thirteen

The revolving carousel, the loud music and the flashing lights made Addy's head spin. It all seemed like a dream, being there, having fun and laughing with Gideon. She felt younger and more carefree than she had in years, and for the first time ever, she felt pretty. He made her feel pretty.

Addy knew that her parents wouldn't approve of riding the merry-go-round, but she didn't care. If they chastised her, she would gladly accept her responsibility and listen dutifully to their reasoning. But for once, she wanted to do something wild and unexpected.

The sounds and smells of the carnival

added to her excitement: the shrieks of children on the spinning rides, the shouts of the barkers, the sizzle of frying hamburgers, the odors of hot buttered popcorn mingling with candy apples, pizza and the slightly oily smell of metal gears and creaking machinery. High above the carousel, she caught glimpses of a multicolored hot-air balloon, its swaying basket filled with merrymakers.

"Catch the ring!" Gideon said. He pointed toward a wooden arm that jutted out from a tall blue-and-yellow-painted pole. "See!" he called as they approached it.

She reached for the silvery circle, but when the merry-go-round swept her past it, her mount went down, putting the ring out of reach. They both laughed.

"I'll get it next time," she promised, watching it over her shoulder.

Up and down, round and round her make-believe horse with the flowing mane and tail carried her, seeming to leaving a trail of organ music and lights behind her. She completed the rotation again; Addy stood in the stirrups and reached up and out. This time she clasped the glittering ring.

To her surprise, it was light, too light to be metal, only plastic. Still, Addy was pleased with herself that she'd caught it, and Gideon seemed to think that she'd achieved some marvelous feat.

"You got it!" Gideon congratulated her as his hand settled over hers on the horse's reins.

Addy blushed. Was he holding her hand? In public? She glanced around to see if anyone had noticed, but she didn't pull her hand away. It felt too good.

"There's another," Gideon cried.

The horse she was riding rose as the arm with the ring swept closer. Addy held her breath...and yes! She stretched as far as she could and grabbed the ring. "Got it!" she cried triumphantly. "And this one isn't silver. It's gold!"

Gideon laughed. "That means you win another ride," he explained. "Catch the *brass* ring, and you're a winner."

"Really? I won? I won!"

He was still laughing. "You won."

A troubling thought crossed her mind, and she suddenly grew serious. "Is it gambling? It isn't gambling, is it?" Gambling went against the *ordnung*. Riding the merry-go-round was one thing, a minor transgression, but she couldn't be a part of gambling.

"Ne," Gideon assured her as the carousel slowed and the music wound down. "No more than playing at corn toss and winning a prize. I paid for the ride, not the chance to win another. But you did catch the brass ring." His endearing grin widened. "Do you want to ride again?"

She felt like she was smiling so hard that her cheeks might shatter. "Only if you'll ride the tiger," she dared.

He did, and the second ride was as thrilling as the first. This time, neither of them caught the brass ring, but it didn't matter. The merry-go-round was crowded, and everyone seemed to be having as much fun as she was. Addy didn't see any other Amish people riding the carousel animals, but there was a young Mennonite couple, the woman in a small lace *kapp* and a chubby toddler in his father's backpack riding what looked like a pink sleigh. The woman smiled at her, and Addy smiled back, sharing the happiness of the carousel and the day.

The second ride was ending when Addy heard a familiar, high-pitched voice calling out to her. She looked up to see Ellie, Thomas, Sara and two other Amish couples walking toward the merry-go-round. Ellie was waving frantically.

"Gideon." Addy pointed. "It's Sara and Ellie. I think they might be looking for you."

"Not time to meet up yet. I've still got an hour. Come on!" He caught Addy's hand and tugged, leading her away.

Addy had to run to keep up with him. They jumped off the far side of the carousel and ran past a balloon stand and a ring-toss booth. They dodged a man in a clown suit and hurried down an aisle between a pretzel seller and an exhibit with signs boasting of the world's largest horse.

"Gideon! Stop. Someone will see us," she called to him. She was laughing, though why, she didn't know. "We shouldn't be running. What will people think?"

Laughing with her, Gideon stopped short and dodged between two flaps in a big tent.

Addy blinked, her eyes slowly becoming adjusted to the semidarkness after the bright light of the July sunshine. The tent was being used for storage for the nearby food vendors; she spotted stacks of plastic trays with hot-dog rolls and canisters of sodas for fountains.

"Addy." Gideon wasn't laughing now, and his voice was husky. He stepped closer and put his arms around her.

It seemed the most natural thing in the world for Addy to look up at him. Then to meet his kiss. Their lips touched, tentatively, gently, and then with a sweetness that sent a rush of warmth from the tips of her toes to the crown of her head. In an instant, Addy felt enveloped in his strength and solid steadiness, and it felt so right that it brought tears to her eyes.

She moved back out of his embrace. "Oh, Gideon," she murmured. "What have you done?" She could still feel the heady thrill of his arms around her.

"*Ne*, Addy, it's not what *I've* done," he said. "It's what *you've* done. To me." He took a deep breath and exhaled slowly. "You know, you're the first girl I've ever kissed."

"I am?" She stared at him, thinking that might have been the most surprising thing anyone had ever said to her.

Was it possible? Popular Gideon, with the girls crowding around him, Gideon who never walked or rode home from a singing alone, had never kissed a girl? He was as inexperienced in kissing as she was? And then, in spite of herself, she gave a small chuckle. *Less,* she thought. *Less, because I kissed Joseph.*

She swallowed, trying to reason what kind of fast woman she was, kissing young men right and left. But oh, now she knew that there were kisses and then *there were kisses*, and what she and Joseph shared was no kiss at all compared to what had just happened between her and Gideon.

Addy's knees were weak, and it felt as if doves' wings fluttered in her chest. She thought she should say something else to him, but no words came. She just stood there, looking up at him, feeling the wonder of the moment.

"*Ya*, the only woman I've ever kissed, if you don't count the girls in primary school when I was too young to know what I was doing." He chuckled. "And the only woman I've ever asked to marry me."

"Marry you?" Addy shivered, suddenly cold despite the heat in the still and dusty tent. "You want to marry me?"

He looked at her as if she had said the silliest thing. "What do you think I was talking about on your roof the other night? Forget courting. We've already had our courting. I know you better than any woman I've ever known, and I'm more sure of this than anything I've ever been sure of." He caught her hand, brought it to his lips and kissed her knuckles. "Addy Coblentz, will you do me the honor of becoming my wife?"

"I...I..." she stammered. She looked up at him, tears suddenly coming to her eyes. What would her *mam* think? "I..." She gazed up at his beautiful face and...

Yanking her hand out of his, she turned and fled through the open tent flap.

"Addy!" Gideon called after her. "Addy? What's wrong? Come back!"

Addy ran. She didn't know why, but she did. She darted back onto the midway, into the milling crowd, making herself as small as possible as she made her escape.

She had to find her mother.

For more than an hour, Addy hunted for her parents, searching the sheep barn and the 4-H building, walking up and down the aisles between the food tents and the farm exhibits. She returned to the horse barn and the flower displays. Twice, she was certain the tall Amish woman walking ahead of her with a shorter man was her mother and father, but each time she was disappointed when the couples turned out to be someone else.

Finally, Addy spotted Anna coming away from a stand that sold cotton candy. Anna was with her two stepsons, the red-haired twins. One of the boys was carrying their little sister, Rose. Addy called to them and asked if any of them had seen her parents.

"I did," Rudy said. "They were looking for you. Preacher Reuben said that he thought you might be in the Conservation Hall. Your mother said that she'd had enough of the fair and was ready to go home as soon as they found you."

Addy thanked him and made her way quickly toward the building. If she'd missed them again, she'd go back to the van. She didn't know where else to look. But this time, she was successful. She found her parents sitting under the trees beside a portable fish pond, just to the left of the concrete-block Conservation Hall. Her father was drinking lemonade.

Her mother glanced up and saw her coming. "There you are," she said. "We were worried about you. We couldn't imagine where you'd gotten to."

"I'm sorry." Addy sank onto the bench beside her mother. The water looked cool and inviting, with the orange-and-black fish swimming around. A small waterfall at one end kept the current in the rock-lined pool swirling gently. "But I'm glad I found you." She took a breath. "Because I need to talk to you," she said. "About something important." She looked around, glad that the three of them were alone here with the fish, glad that she could say what she needed to before she burst with what was pent up inside her.

"I hope you haven't found something foolish you want to buy," her mother said peevishly. "Someone is selling tomatoes they've grown upside down from hanging baskets, over by the tractors. Can you imagine that anyone would think they could grow decent tomatoes that way? And to pay twenty dollars for a single tomato plant in a plastic—"

"*Mam*, please," Addy interrupted. "I need you to listen to me." And they were going to have to listen. Because she was only going to say this once. She gathered her courage. "You know that I love and respect you both. No one could have better parents."

Her mother's eyes narrowed. "When a girl says such a thing, it usually means trouble," she pronounced. "What are you saying, *Dorcas*? Do you want to leave the church? Turn Mennonite and become a missionary like your cousin Leah?"

"Martha." Her father frowned at her mother. "How can you say such a thing? Listen to the girl. What is it, Dorcas?"

"Addy," she said quietly. "I'm Addy, *Dat*."

"Well, go ahead," her mother said, making a show of folding her hands and placing them in her lap. "Speak your piece, since you've made such a fuss about it."

"I can't do what you ask," Addy blurted. "I've tried to follow your wishes, but I can't.

About choosing a husband." Her gaze moved from her father's face to her mother's. All the sounds around her seemed to dissipate as she spoke. "There's someone I care about deeply...someone I love." She took another breath. "And he's asked me to be his wife."

"Who?" her mother demanded. "Don't tell me he's an *Englisher.*"

Addy stared at her mother. "I would never leave my faith. Do you not know me any better than that, *Mam*?"

"Then who?" Her father fixed her with a compassionate gaze. "Do we know him?"

"Gideon. Gideon Esch."

Her mother shot up off the bench, her face turning first pale and then a purple-red. "Sara Yoder's hired hand? Have you lost your senses? Haven't you heard a thing we've told you?"

"Ach, ach." Her father rocked back and forth, tugging at his beard. "Such a thing when we had such hopes for you."

"I'm sorry," Addy said. And then she shook her head again. *"Ne,* actually, I'm not sorry.

Gideon is a good man. I love him, and he loves me. And he wants to marry me. *Mam*, *Dat*, I've waited what seems like my whole life for this man and…I won't let him go."

Her father took off his hat and rested it on his knee. He ran his fingers through his thinning hair and hung his head. "I don't know, I don't know," he muttered. "There will be Sara's match to pay for, and however will we manage that?"

"Do you have any idea how much that is?" her mother asked her.

And then she named a number that made Addy's stomach turn over.

"So much?" Addy breathed.

"Didn't I make it clear to you that you had to find a husband who could afford Sara's fee?" Her mother's mouth tightened into a thin white line.

Addy only thought for a minute before she looked at her mother again. "So, we'll pay it," she said firmly. "Gideon and me. We'll work until we can raise that amount. You won't have to bear the burden, I promise.

We'll work for years if we have to, but I won't give him up. If he's willing, I'll wait for him. We're going to be married."

"And you don't think that we know more about life than a green girl who's been no farther than Dover, who knows nothing of the world, and of marriage? If you choose to go your own willful way, you can expect no help from us."

"You know that your mother and I love you," her father said. "You'll always be our daughter. But we don't want to see you rush into a difficult life with a hired hand. You can understand that, can't you? You've known this Wisconsin fellow, what, a month? Two? Don't be in such a hurry to set your feet on a rocky path."

"*Ya*, a poor boy," her mother repeated with a shake of her finger. "A hired man with no trade, no land and no prospects, who will be making sausages in someone else's kitchen and selling them off the back porch for the rest of your life!"

Chapter Fourteen

The following morning, Addy hurried across the pasture toward Sara's house before the dew had burned away in the midsummer sunshine. Breakfast with her parents had been tense, their only communication with her having been "Pass the butter" from her father, and "I suppose you're still bent on this foolishness with that boy" from her mother. Remaining respectful to her parents, Addy had held her tongue. She cleared away and washed the breakfast dishes in record time, left them draining on the counter and headed out of the house.

Truthfully, Addy hadn't even been all that

worried about her parents that morning. All she could think about was Gideon. She'd left him so abruptly the previous day after he'd proposed to her. What if he'd changed his mind? Or if he'd asked her to marry him in the heady confusion of their first kiss?

Addy's heart swelled as she thought of that kiss, gentle as the touch of a butterfly's wing, and as stirring as sunrise over her father's fields. *I love him,* she thought. *This is what love feels like.* She'd heard girls say that being in love made you weak and woozy, positively giddy, but this morning, she'd never felt more clearheaded and determined. Everything seemed brighter, the grass greener, the clouds whiter and the sweet smell of the earth richer and more intense. She'd never felt gladder to be alive. It was all she could do not to burst into a hymn of thanksgiving.

As Addy climbed over the new stile, her thoughts fell to Sara. She wondered how Sara would feel about not getting her matchmaking fee, at least not for a while. Surely, she'd understand. Addy and Gideon would pay her fee; it just might take a while.

Then she wondered if Gideon might want to return to Wisconsin to get a better job and earn more than the small wage he was being paid at Sara's, due to the fact that she was providing room and board. After all, he no longer needed Sara's matchmaking services. If Gideon did need to go to Wisconsin, how would she survive without seeing him...without seeing his broad grin or hearing his laughter? It was so strange to think that she'd only known him two months, yet it felt as though she'd been waiting for him all her life.

The sound of hammering broke through Addy's thoughts. She stopped and looked around, gauging the direction of the sound. It was early. Had Gideon finished his breakfast and started on the new pasture fence already? Sara had just purchased an additional twelve acres from a neighbor and had mentioned that she wanted to run sheep in the meadow beyond the woodlot. It had to be Gideon at work; Sara and Ellie certainly wouldn't be out beating nails with a hammer.

Addy turned away from the house, in the direction of the hammering. She hurried down the faint track that led past a row of four beehives. The rutted lane wound through the towering hardwoods where Gideon had recently cut down a lightning-struck maple, through a shaded tunnel of greenery, to a three-acre clearing on the far side. Immediately, she caught sight of one of Sara's mules standing patiently beside a new line of fence posts. More posts and a roll of stock wire were stacked on the farm wagon, and just beyond, a bare-chested Gideon was heaving a heavy wooden post into the ground.

Addy stopped, clapped a hand over her mouth and stared in astonishment. She could never remember seeing a grown Amish man without his shirt. The English, certainly. She'd seen them flaunting their bodies at the beach and sometimes while mowing a lawn, but her father had certainly never shed his shirt in hot weather. Not only was Gideon shirtless, but his head was bare, too, his buttery-blond hair falling nearly to his shoulders and shiny in the sunlight.

Addy knew that she should turn away, that no decent, unmarried girl would ogle a man. But, as she had the first time she'd laid eyes on Gideon Esch, she was struck by his beauty. Surely, any God who could make a man thus couldn't blame her for admiring His work.

For a few moments, Addy just stood there, unashamed, watching Gideon and dreaming of what might be. What had she done to deserve such happiness? And how was it possible that Gideon would come so far from his own home to find her here in Seven Poplars and ask her to be his wife? Surely, this was God's hand at work.

She smiled. *I love this man,* she thought. *God willing, he and I will marry and create our own home.* She could see them working side by side in the garden, breaking bread and a simple meal together at the kitchen table, and kneeling for prayer together at the end of a long day.

Gideon turned back toward the wagon. A flush heated Addy's cheeks, and her heartbeat quickened. Had he caught her watching him? She stepped back into the shadows of the trees, but not before Jasper raised his head and snorted in her direction.

"Addy!" Gideon grabbed his shirt off the wagon bed, turned his back to her and hastily pulled it on. Seizing his straw hat, he clamped it over his bare head and strode toward her. "Addy, don't you dare run."

She wanted to. Because now she *did* feel light-headed. And scared. But when he got closer, she couldn't stop from reaching her hands out to him.

Gideon took her slender hands in his large and powerful ones and looked into her eyes. "I've been waiting for you. I didn't sleep a wink last night, for thinking about you. Missing you."

Instantly, the image of her standing in Sara's yard in the moonlight, throwing stones at *his* window made her giggle. "Gideon, " she managed. "Did you think I'd come here in the middle of the night?" His eyes were shining, his slightly crooked grin so endearing that it made her want to weep with joy.

"You scared me when you ran away at the fair yesterday. I was afraid you—"

"I had to think." Was he going to kiss her again? Just the thought of the moment they'd shared in the tent made her blush. But she couldn't allow such a thing. Not now, not until they… She swallowed. He mustn't believe that she gave her kisses so easily.

"You had to think. Of course you did, Addy."

Her name on his lips made goose bumps rise on the nape of her neck. She loved the sound of it, the way he pronounced it. Addy was who she was now, who she should be and she had him to thank for it all.

No, changing her name had been Gideon's suggestion, but *she* had been the one to change who she was. And the woman she was now deserved to be happy, with a good man. She deserved a home, a husband and, if it was God's plan, children to love and teach and care for.

She inhaled deeply and the clean, wholesome scent of a hardworking man filled her head. She glimpsed the sprinkling of golden hairs on Gideon's broad chest where he'd not yet fastened all the buttons of his shirt. She was all too aware of the lines of sinewy muscle of his powerful shoulders and upper arms, and she could feel his strong hands holding hers. And she knew, perhaps for the first time, the intensity of a woman's attraction to a man.

And with that realization, all the teachings of her faith came flooding back to her. Gently, she freed herself from Gideon's grasp and stepped back. When he reached for her, she halted him with a gesture.

"*Ne*, Gideon," she cautioned. She clasped her hands behind her back to hide her trembling. "No more of that. We have to do this right. I won't bring shame to our parents or ourselves."

He smiled at her. "So you're saying yes? You'll be my wife?"

"I'm sorry I ran away yesterday. I was just…a little overwhelmed." She chuckled. "It was so sudden. I didn't…"

"Sudden?" His gaze grew tender. "You knew how I felt about you. *You* were the one who told *me*."

"Please don't remind me." She smiled shyly, then found the courage to meet his gaze again. "You told everyone you weren't going to take a wife. Not for years."

"You changed everything. Including me."

She clenched her hands together tightly. "Maybe we both changed."

They were both quiet for a moment and then he said, "I hope I didn't frighten you yesterday, when I kissed you."

"Did I seem frightened to you? *Ne*, I really did need to think. And I had to talk to my mother and father." Her smile faded. "They aren't pleased. They won't give their blessing because they wanted me to choose a man who…"

"Was more than a hired hand?" he finished for her.

She nodded. "But you know I don't care about that. It doesn't matter to me. You're all that matters. I'll go with you back to Wisconsin if you want—maybe you can hire on at a farm there. If you're willing to marry without my parents' blessing, I am."

"Willing?" His beautiful gray eyes glistened with emotion. "What have I been saying? I want you to be my wife. I want to provide for you, take care of you. I want us to be a family."

"And you would promise to live according to the laws of our church and raise our children in the faith?"

"*Ya*, of course. What else would we do? If God grants us the blessing of children, it would be our duty and our joy."

She reached for his hand. "My parents can't afford to pay Sara's fee. I'll have to work and earn that myself. You understand that, don't you? And it might take a long time."

His eyes narrowed as he looked into her

face. "And it really doesn't matter to you if I'm as poor as Job's turkey?"

"The wealth of a man isn't to be counted in money. It's what's in his heart and character."

"I think you mean that."

"I do," she said.

Gideon bent his head as if to kiss her, and she laid two fingers on his lips. "No more of that," she said. "We still have much to settle before we get to any more kissing."

"Which is important," he said, chuckling. "For you are a woman with lips made to be kissed."

"By a *husband*," she answered. "Not by a cut-up charmer with a reputation for chasing every pretty girl in the county."

Gideon groaned. "Why do I think that being married to you will not be easy?"

She laughed. "You can still change your mind."

"It's taken me thirty years to find the right woman." He took her other hand. "I'm not going to let you get away so easily." He laid his cheek against her forehead. "But I want your parents' blessing, Addy. I already have mine."

She looked up at him in astonishment. "You do?"

"*Ya. Dat* starts his sausage-making early. I walked to the chair shop and called him on the telephone this morning." He shrugged. "My mother was there helping him, so I spoke to her, too. They were happy to hear the news. My mother was so happy, she cried." He shrugged again. "*Mam* always cries when she is most happy."

Addy wasn't sure whether to be pleased or put out. "You were so sure that I would agree to marry you?" she asked. Then she said, "Wait. I don't understand. Your father has a telephone?"

"Not in our house, of course. In the place where he does his work."

"Ah, like the chair shop." She nodded. Telephones were a necessary evil in a place of business. Amish shop owners got dispensations from the church elders to have phones there.

"So I've spoken to my father, and now I have to go and speak to yours," Gideon pronounced. "The sooner, the better."

"It's no use," she said. "He won't change his mind. My mother won't let him."

Gideon arched a blond eyebrow quizzically. "Your mother is the head of the house?"

"I'm afraid so," Addy admitted.

"Mine, too. But I don't think my father knows that yet." He kissed her hand and let go before she could snatch it from him. "Go back to Sara's and wait for me."

"You don't want me to come with you?"

Gideon shook his head. "*Ne*, best I do this alone." He gave her a mischievous look. "Another kiss before I go? A real kiss?"

She shook her head firmly. "I believe you've had enough kissing."

"Even for a newly betrothed couple?"

"*Especially* for a newly betrothed couple."

Addy was cleaning the windows in Sara's parlor when Gideon returned from her parents'. She wanted to run to him, to ask what had happened. She was dying to know what he'd said to her father and if he had said anything hopeful to Gideon. But Gideon had gone straight to Sara, and the two had retreated to the back porch.

Addy dropped her sponge into the bucket and went to the kitchen. She'd not said anything to Sara about the betrothal because she'd thought it better for the two of them to approach her together with the news. Ellie wasn't there; she'd gone to the schoolhouse to check on some work being done on the cloakroom. Addy wished she was, though. Having her friend there would have made things easier.

Addy dumped the bucket into the sink and washed out the sponge. From the porch, she could hear the murmur of voices: Sara's higher one and Gideon's deeper, but she couldn't make out what they were saying. She wasn't normally a busybody, but she strained to hear. A few more words passed between them, then, to her surprise, Sara laughed.

A minute later, Gideon came into the kitchen. "Addy." He smiled at her.

"Did my father agree to give us his blessing?" she asked.

Gideon grimaced. "Those were not *exactly* the words he used."

She looked to Sara. "I'll pay every penny of your fee. You have my word on it. I can understand if you wouldn't want me to go on working here for you, but—"

"Did I say that?" Sara asked, cutting her off. "Don't put words in my mouth. Are you dissatisfied with your wages or what I've asked you to do?"

"*Ne*, but…"

Sara folded her arms. "Have I asked you for money?" She seemed more formidable than ever this morning in her sturdy black shoes and stockings, her dark purple dress and spotless white apron.

"*Ne*, but—"

"Have a little faith, girl, that I know what I'm doing." She looked Addy up and down. "You have dirt on your nose, and your *kapp*...." She sighed. "Get a clean *kapp* and apron from my room. Your parents are on their way here, and I need you to look presentable, not like some hired girl."

"My mother and father are coming here?" She looked to Gideon. "Now?"

Gideon laughed. "*Ya*, now. So you best hurry. Your father was hitching up his buggy when I left his farmyard. I made Jasper trot all the way home, but they won't be far behind me."

"You need to change into your white shirt and church trousers, as well," Sara ordered Gideon. "When I hold a meeting with a girl's parents, I expect the young man to be presentable." She clapped her hands. "Now. Go. Off with you both!"

Completely bewildered, Addy hurried to do as Sara had asked. She couldn't imagine what Sara could possibly say to her mother and father that would convince them to approve of the match. Would she guarantee Gideon's employment? Promise that the two of them would have jobs until they'd raised the fees? Addy doubted that that would make a difference to her mother. Gideon would still be poor and landless. As much as she wanted her parents' blessing for her marriage, she knew just how intractable her mother could be, especially when she believed she was in the right.

Heart in her throat, Addy rushed to wash up, pin her hair up under a fresh *kapp* and don a starched white apron. Neither Ellie's shoes nor Sara's would fit her, so she was forced to wash her bare feet and go into the parlor as she was.

Her mother and father were already there. Her mother had taken the time to put her cape on, and her black bonnet over her prayer *kapp*. Both were stern-faced and seemed nervous. Only Sara was at ease, dressed as Addy had last seen her in the kitchen. Her only compromise was that she had traded her blue scarf for a white *kapp*, starched and ironed to a standard that even Addy's mother couldn't criticize.

Sara waved Addy to a straight-backed chair

and then turned her attention back to Addy's mother and father. "Would you like hot tea? Coffee? Or would you prefer something cold to drink?" She asked as she passed them a plate of small, frosted cakes.

Addy's mother refused the sweets and stated that she wasn't thirsty. Addy noticed that her father reached for a cake, then drew his hand back quickly when her mother scowled at him. "This is a waste of time, cousin," her mother said. "We do not approve of this Gideon, and nothing you or he could possibly say will change our minds."

"But your daughter is of age," Sara said calmly. "And she has stated that she is willing to have the young man to husband, for richer or poorer."

Addy's mother threw a black look at her father. When he didn't speak, she said, "We can't stop her from marrying, but we can refuse to approve of it. They have nothing, will have nothing and will struggle all their lives. It's not what we would have for our daughter." Her mouth tightened. "And I'm surprised that you, Sara, who have a reputation as something of a matchmaker, could sanction such a poor match."

"Frankly," her father said as he reached for a frosted cake, and this time took a piece, "we don't have the money to pay your fee, so we couldn't give it to you if we did approve."

Addy felt a hand on her shoulder and looked up to find Gideon standing behind her chair. "My father will pay Addy's fee and mine," he said.

Addy glanced up at him, hope making her giddy. "He will? He...would...could do that?" she stammered.

Gideon grinned. "Sara, maybe an explanation would come easier from you."

"*Ya*, it might," Sara said. "Perhaps you would like that tea now? I find that almost any situation is easier to explain over a cup of tea."

"I'm listening," Addy's mother said. Addy's father's eyes were wide, his mouth full of cake.

Sara smiled. "Gideon's financial situation

is not quite what it seems. When his parents asked me to find a bride for him, they expressed concern that some families might wish to make an alliance with him because of the sausage."

Addy's father choked, and her mother patted him on the back. He wiped his mouth with the back of his hand. "Maybe I will have that tea," he rasped.

"Of course, Preacher Reuben. Addy, would you mind fetching the tea tray? It's already brewed."

Addy rose hesitantly. She didn't want to miss a word of this, but she could hardly refuse.

"I'll help you," Gideon offered. Together they walked to the kitchen.

"What's this all about?" she whispered. "Sausage? What does that mean?"

"It means my father is well-off," he said ruefully. "His business is…substantial."

"But you said… I thought he sold sausage to his neighbors to get by."

"Once, years ago, but then his business

took off. Esch's Sausage. I can't believe you haven't heard of it. They sell it in the *Englisher* supermarkets all over Wisconsin. And in his shops."

"Shops. He has more than one?" She sank into a chair, unable to believe what she was hearing. Gideon wasn't a penniless hired man? She had seen the ads for Esch's Sausage in *The Budget*, but she'd never made the connection. What had the ad said? "Best-selling Amish sausage in three states"?

"He has three stores. Four, if I open one, as he has been asking me to. It's what I was thinking. If you agree, of course. Not to go back to Wisconsin, but to open a store here in Kent County. I can see how close you are to your parents, and I wouldn't wish to take you away from them and all your friends. And I thought maybe we might expand to sell some of that wonderful scrapple you make?"

"So all this time you've been deceiving everyone, making them think you were poor?" She knew she should be angry with him for not telling the truth, but all she could think was that his father would pay Sara's fee, and they would be free to marry.

"I didn't lie to you," he said.

"But why?" She could hardly get the words out. "Why make everyone think that you were poor?"

"It's like Sara said. In my hometown, some mothers wanted their daughters to marry with me because of my father's success. Once, I almost asked a girl to be my wife, but I found out that it was only for the money. She didn't love me. It was the thought of being the wife to the heir to Esch's Sausage. I was badly hurt by that, and so were my parents. They didn't want that to happen again, so my mother and Sara put their heads together. If I *did* fall in love and the young woman was willing to take me for richer or poorer, then it would prove that it was a good match, a match that would make us both happy." He grinned at her. "Am I forgiven?"

"Did you love her? This Wisconsin girl

who wanted to marry the son of the sausage king?"

"*Ne*. I thought I did, but it was more my pride that was injured than my heart. It wasn't until I met you that I realized what real love is."

She tried not to smile, not wanting to let him off the hook so easily. "And if I did say yes, when would we marry?"

"Sara said that usually weddings are held in November here, but I would be willing… *Ne*, I would like very much to marry you as soon as the banns could be read."

"Three or four weeks, at least. Not before early October, surely," she said. "If I agree."

"You already agreed," he argued.

"So ask me again."

He took a step closer to her. "My beautiful Addy, will you be my wife?"

She sighed. "I suppose I must. Because without me, who would keep you on the straight and narrow? And who else would put up with you?"

"You will?" He stood and pulled her into

his arms and kissed her soundly. "You will marry me, Addy? Truly?"

She circled his strong neck with her arms and stood on tiptoe to return his kiss. *"Ya,"* she murmured. "I will."

"Addy!" Her mother's shocked voice cut through her haze of happiness. She stood in the doorway. *"Vas* is this?"

"Oh, hush, woman," her father admonished in his best preaching voice. "Don't be foolish. It's only natural that they share a little kiss. They've just become betrothed." He crossed the kitchen and slapped Gideon on the back. "Welcome to the family, son."

Sara rested her fists on her hips and looked from Addy and Gideon to Addy's mother. "Well, cousin, what do you say now? Will you give your blessing to this match?"

Her mother's mouth puckered and then her expression softened. "I suppose we'll have to, considering what we've just witnessed. It's either that, or risk losing our daughter's reputation in the community altogether."

Sara began to chuckle, and soon they were

all laughing together. But Gideon never let go of Addy's hand, and she never stopped smiling because somehow, against all odds, Sara had found the perfect match for her. And in the blink of an eye, all of Addy's dreams had come true.

Epilogue

Cashton, Wisconsin, Autumn

Addy carried the duck-shaped tureen of potato soup to the small round table in front of the window. Already waiting was a covered plate of roast chicken, a loaf of still-warm rye bread, an assortment of cheese and a delicious Dutch slaw that Gideon's mother had sent over. A Brown Betty pudding that Addy had made herself from his *grossmama*'s recipe bubbled in a kettle on the hearth.

It was Addy's favorite time of the day. She put on a clean apron and opened the cabin door. "Gideon, supper."

"Coming!" he shouted.

Just beyond where her husband stood, on the sturdy wooden dock, a pair of wild ducks circled overhead. Smiling as she pulled her sweater closer around her shoulders, Addy watched as the ducks dropped onto the smooth surface of the blue-green water. The hardwoods were turning red and gold, and sundown brought crisp air and a promise of winter.

Although she had to admit she was just a tiny bit homesick, Addy would miss Wisconsin when they returned to Kent County from their honeymoon. In the weeks they'd spent here, visiting Gideon's parents, sisters, aunts and uncles and grandparents, she'd been welcomed into more homes than she could count on the fingers of both hands.

She'd always wanted a sister; now she had eight of them, all plump and blonde and merry. They looked so much alike that sometimes she had trouble telling them apart. Everyone wanted to meet her, and every sister had advice for dealing with Gideon and curbing his ways, but beneath the teasing, it was clear that they all dearly loved him. And her mother-in-law had turned out to be kind and sensible, much like her Aunt Hannah.

Addy would miss them all. Her thoughts were a tumble of new sights and sounds, new hymns, new friends and new recipes. And she would certainly miss this rustic two-hundred-year-old log house that was their first home together, the place where she and Gideon had truly become man and wife.

When they had first arrived in Wisconsin, Addy had expected that they'd stay at his parents' home or at least with a relative. But no. Gideon had surprised her with this delightful two-room cabin on a lake, far enough from the home farmhouse to give the newlyweds privacy.

Mornings, they would rise from their snug bedroom and walk across the fields to breakfast with one of his sisters and her family. Then she and Gideon would go their separate ways, he to consult with his father and brothers-in-law, to form plans for the Kent

County sausage shop or to help out in the plant, and she to work in the nearest family store. There, Gideon's sisters had shown her how to run the register and wait on customers. Gideon explained that when they returned to Delaware, the front of the store would be her responsibility. They would hire a counter girl to help her, but Addy would be a real partner in the business.

Midday dinners were always with the extended family and most afternoons for visiting, or sightseeing, or simply taking their ease fishing or boating on the broad, tree-lined lake. But evenings were for her and Gideon alone. Every day at about five o'clock, a sister or a nephew or brother-in-law would pull up in a horse-drawn cart with already-prepared food for their supper.

After their supper, Gideon would light a fire in the fireplace, and the two of them would spend the evening sitting in front of the hearth, playing hearts or Dutch Blitz at the table in front of the window overlooking the lake. There they would watch loons, otters and waterfowl. Sometimes, Gideon would drape one of his jackets around her shoulders and they would walk hand in hand around the shore of the lake.

Other nights, they would put on their sleeping clothes and sit in front of the hearth popping corn in a long-handled popper over the open fire. Then Gideon would heat cider in a copper pan that had been handed down in the Esch family for generations, a pan that some said had come across the ocean from the Old Country long ago. There was no modern cooking stove in the cabin, but they needed none, because this was the *braut haus*, the bride house, where it was customary for Esch couples to spend time alone getting to know each other, rather than cooking and cleaning.

Addy saw Gideon walking down the path toward the cabin, and she couldn't wait to be with him. She crossed the log porch and hurried down the rough stone steps. "Your supper's going to get cold if you don't hurry along," she called in an attempt to hide her eagerness. "No fish?"

"None tonight." He propped his fishing pole against a porch post, caught her around the waist and swung her around.

"Gideon!" she squealed. "What if someone comes?"

"Then they might see this." He lowered her to the porch and kissed her. "Or this." And he swept her up in his arms and carried her into the house.

"Gideon, put me down," she protested. Secretly, she was thrilled when he acted so outrageously. Her heart thumped so loud against her ribs that it was a wonder they couldn't hear it all the way in his mother's kitchen. "Our supper... The soup will get cold."

"Woman, you're getting as bad as my sisters."

He released her, and she tucked her hands behind her back to keep them from straying to his face. She loved to stroke his cheek or the swell of his shoulder. How strange that such a short time ago, to touch him was wrong, but now it was right. So long as they were alone, they could hug or kiss. It was a benefit of marriage that had never occurred to her.

"I was thinking that if the *braut haus* is just for brides and grooms, that means that we can never stay here again," she said with a sigh. The idea made her sad because she realized that perhaps never again would she have Gideon all to herself.

"Ne." He grinned. "It's tradition, but not a rule. If you like, whenever we visit, we'll stay here, us and our ten children."

"Ten?" She giggled. She hoped she would have boys and girls with butter-yellow hair and Gideon's beautiful gray eyes, but secretly, she didn't want them just yet. In God's time, of course. What He sent and when He sent them, she would open her arms and heart to them. But there was so much for her and Gideon to do…a new house to build… the sausage to make…the shop to be opened.

"Well, we can start with one or two girls," Gideon declared, taking her hand to lead her inside. "Girls are better help when there's a lot of children. Boys just want to sneak off and go fishing."

"You would know better than me," she teased.

He grinned. "Whether there are two of us or twelve, we'll come back to visit our Esch family together. We can bring your parents with us, if you like."

Addy's eyes narrowed. Was he serious? Bring her mother here to this lake cabin? Put her mother and his mother together in the same kitchen? "Maybe sometime," she hedged.

"Maybe a long, long time from now, we'll bring them," he said. "If it pleases you." His voice deepened. "But for now I like having you all to myself." He drew her into his arms again and kissed her tenderly. "I think I like having a wife very much."

"And I like having a husband," she admitted, looking up at him.

"So if you like me so much, can I have kissing before soup?"

"Wash the lake off your hands," she instructed, trying to sound stern. "And sit down. I'll not have a nice meal wasted with your silliness."

And they did eat the supper his sisters had brought, but not the pudding, because when Addy remembered it later, it had burned to the bottom of the kettle, and it was far too late for anything but kissing and sweet, shared laughter.

* * * * *

Dear Reader,

Welcome to my new Love Inspired series, The Amish Matchmaker. A part of me was sad to leave the Hannah's Daughters series behind. But now that Hannah's cousin, Sara Yoder, has come to Seven Poplars, I couldn't be more excited!

Among the Plain people, arranged marriages aren't as unusual as one might think. They believe that faith and family are the most important things in life, and that with God, all things are possible. Doesn't everyone, young or old, plain or beautiful, deserve a chance at happiness? So how can finding that special someone sometimes be so difficult? Everyone values honesty, kindness and hard work, but we all have faults and burrs that may need polishing.

That's where Sara comes in. She's a good judge of character who knows how to bring the right couples together, but she also gives sage advice to her potential brides and grooms. Some say that Sara has never met a candidate she couldn't match, even the most difficult cases. And that's why romance and love have come to Seven Poplars, Amish style. Happy reading!

Your friend,
Emma Miller

REQUEST YOUR FREE BOOKS!

2 FREE RIVETING INSPIRATIONAL NOVELS IN TRUE LARGE PRINT PLUS 2 FREE MYSTERY GIFTS

Love Inspired®
SUSPENSE

TRUE LARGE PRINT

YES! Please send me 2 FREE Love Inspired® Suspense True Large Print novels and my 2 FREE mystery gifts (gifts are worth about $10). After receiving them, if I don't wish to receive any more books, I can return the shipping statement marked "cancel." If I don't cancel, I will receive 3 brand-new true large print novels every month and be billed just $7.99 per book in the U.S. or $9.99 per book in Canada. That's a savings of at least 20% off the cover price. It's quite a bargain! Shipping and handling is just 50¢ per book in the U.S. and 75¢ per book in Canada.* I understand that accepting the 2 free books and gifts places me under no obligation to buy anything. I can always return the shipment and cancel at any time. Even if I never buy another book, the two free books and gifts are mine to keep forever.

124/324 IDN F5GD

Name	(PLEASE PRINT)

Address	Apt. #

City	State/Prov.	Zip/Postal Code

Signature (if under 18, a parent or guardian must sign)

Mail to the Harlequin® Reader Service:
IN U.S.A.: P.O. Box 1867, Buffalo, NY 14240-1867
IN CANADA: P.O. Box 609, Fort Erie, Ontario L2A 5X3

* Terms and prices subject to change without notice. Prices do not include applicable taxes. Sales tax applicable in N.Y. Canadian residents will be charged applicable taxes. Offer not valid in Quebec. This offer is limited to one order per household. Not valid for current subscribers to Love Inspired Suspense True Large Print books. All orders subject to credit approval. Credit or debit balances in a customer's account(s) may be offset by any other outstanding balance owed by or to the customer. Please allow 4 to 6 weeks for delivery. Offer available while quantities last.

Your Privacy—The Harlequin® Reader Service is committed to protecting your privacy. Our Privacy Policy is available online at www.ReaderService.com or upon request from the Harlequin Reader Service.

We make a portion of our mailing list available to reputable third parties that offer products we believe may interest you. If you prefer that we not exchange your name with third parties, or if you wish to clarify or modify your communication preferences, please visit us at www.ReaderService.com/consumerschoice or write to us at Harlequin Reader Service Preference Service, P.O. Box 9062, Buffalo, NY 14269. Include your complete name and address.

LISTLP13TRR